I0562087

On Any Given Day

On Any Given Day

Short Slices of Life

Thelma Ellen-Carter

POSITIVE GROWTH & DEVELOPMENT INSTITUTE

Copyright © 2025 by Thelma Ellen-Carter

All rights reserved.

No part of this publication may be reproduced, distributed, or transmitted in any form or by any means, including photocopying, recording, or other electronic or mechanical methods, without the prior written permission of the publisher, except as permitted by U.S. copyright law. For permission requests, contact Positive Growth & Development Institute / Thelma Ellen-Carter @ rosee@ix.netcom.com.

The scanning, uploading, and distribution of this book via the internet or via any other means without permission of the publisher is illegal and punishable by law. Please purchase only authorized electronic editions, and do not participate in or encourage electronic piracy of copyrighted materials. Your support for the author's rights is appreciated.

The stories, all names, characters, and incidents portrayed in this production are fictitious. Exceptions are indicated on the Author's Note page. No identification with actual persons (living or deceased), places, buildings, and products are intended or should be inferred.

Library of Congress Cataloging-in-Publication Data
Ellen-Carter, Thelma
    On Any Given Day : Short Slices of Life
    Summary: A short-story collection that explores humor, satire, and drama in the everyday lives of Christians. From a church van that detours from a shopping trip to a church funeral that briefly spirals out of control. Thelma's entertaining and relatable characters invite readers to find laughter in expected and unexpected life situations.
    979-8-9905320-0-7 (paperback)
    979-8-9905320-1-4 (digital)
    1. Christian—Humorous—short-story fiction. 2. Christian—Satirical—short-story fiction. 3. Christian—Drama—short-story fiction. 4. Short stories. 5. Urban/suburban—short-story fiction.

Unless otherwise noted, scripture references taken from the
New American Standard Bible® (NASB),
Copyright © 1960, 1962, 1963, 1968, 1971, 1972, 1973, 1975, 1977, 1995 by
The Lockman Foundation.
Used by permission.
www.Lockman.org

Book Cover by Barbara Werden
Illustrations by Sophie Appel

1 Edition   2025

Published by the Positive Growth & Development Institute
Houston, Texas
713.721.5047

With Love

For my husband Irvin, son Nicolas, nephew Michael, and niece Erica

In Memory of

My mom Pauline, dad John, sister Carol, brothers John and Jimmy,
and my brother in Christ, Grady

CONTENTS

ACKNOWLEDGMENTS

I am grateful to Barbara Werden and Sophie Appel for excellent design and getting the manuscript publication ready.

Thanks and much appreciation to Karen Medlin for sharing her God-given editorial eyes and extraordinary editing feedback.

We remember our friend and exceptional designer, Barbara Werden, who recently passed. She was an integral part of our publishing team.

Cherranda Smith, Kathy Quinlin, Sylvia Lombard, and Denise Williams: your friendship, listening ears, feedback, and support have been invaluable.

Last but not least, Irvin, my husband: thanks for your love and support. Nicolas, Michael, Erica, Jackie, and Dosha: your loving encouraging words and positivity about this writing project will remain with me forever!

AUTHOR'S NOTE

At home, work, church, restaurants, stores, events, and meetings, both expected and unexpected life experiences occur. Life experiences lead to one or more of the following: laughter, no problems, problems, love, drama, forgiveness, relaxation, conflict, prayers, and fun. These experiences inspired *On Any Given Day,* a collection of fictitious short stories with fictitious characters.

NOT FICTITIOUS

Dr. Nicolas Ellen's books *Every Christian a Counselor* and *Coming to Know and Walk with God* are excellent reads!

Dr. Nathan Stark is a real and excellent physician.

Grady Gaines Douglas's album *The Power of Agape Love* is awesome!

The Vintage Age Van

D r. Swan (the pastor) and the Elder Board (Jones, Smith, Jenkins, and Lewis) had been planning for a year to get a van for the Vintage Age 60+ church members for transportation from their homes to the new church location in Sugar Land.

The four Elders waited excitedly to show the pastor the church's newly donated fifteen-seat passenger van.

Pastor Swan arrived and jumped out of his black Denali. He looked to the left and muttered, "What in the world is that over there on the parking lot?"

He was walking toward the covered van, when Elder Jenkins came running from the church to stop him and yelled, "Hey, Doc! Come in here first before you go over there!"

Pastor Swan shouted back, "Man, what is that covered up over there?"

"Come inside and we'll explain everything," Elder Jenkins insisted.

Pastor Swan looked at Elder Jenkins and said, "Do you remember that song from *The Wiz*?" He pointed to the covered van and started singing "Don't Nobody Bring Me No Bad News."

Elder Smith, holding open the door, was laughing and coughing.

The pastor walked past Elder Smith and said, "I mean every line in that song, and I know you have not stopped smoking. So, what's going on?"

Elder Jones replied, "Doc, good news! An anonymous donor gave the church a new fifteen-passenger van for the Vintage Age members!"

Pastor Swan gasped. "What! Who? How soon can we pay for the tag, title, insurance, and whatever else we need to get this moving?"

Beaming, Elder Jones said, "Doc, all that has been taken care of by the anonymous donor."

"Thank You, God! We are grateful. Let's see it!" Pastor Swan exclaimed.

The four Elders started singing, "Don't Nobody Bring Me No Bad News" as they walked out the church doors behind the pastor.

He turned and said, "Now y'all got singing jokes!"

They all grinned and clapped each other on the back as they strode out to admire the shiny van and revel in the camaraderie of their shared vision.

The 50+ Apartment Evangelism Outreach

Pastor Swan was in the office reading *Every Christian a Counselor*. It brought to his mind the GTJBC (Going To Jesus Bible Church) Evangelism Team's successful outreach at the Seniors 50+ Apartment Complex.

When the GTJBC team had an event to share the gospel at the apartment complex, twenty seniors came to the outreach program. Fourteen accepted Christ. Another attendee was a retired pastor looking for a church. Five of the fifteen who accepted Christ then began attending other churches.

Over the past six months, ten had completed the GTJBC's assimilation seminars and home visits with Pastor Swan and the First Lady Swan. Pastor Swan began smiling and shaking his head from side to side as he remembered the home visits that he and his wife had with each member of the group, now known as Vintage.

He prayed, "God, I know we have asked You to extend our territory. For these ten Seniors, we do thank You. I am asking You to please give our church's Elders, administration team, the entire church body, and me Your wisdom to love and serve this group. Lord, You have given me a great variety of shepherding challenges with these dear ones."

1. Brother John is seventy and a widower. During his home visit he told me and my dear wife Margaret: "Pastor, I have been praying for a wife to pick up where Ruth (who passed two months ago) left off. I need somebody to cook for me, keep this house clean, keep my dentures clean, and keep my toenails cut." Brother John then reached down, took off his bedroom slippers, and said, "Look at these things; they're too long and hurt when I move my feet under the covers or have my shoes on."

2. Brother Jimmy, age seventy-five, said, "Pastor Swan and First Lady, I accepted Christ for me, and I am praying for my sister Emma. I figure if I start living right and stop my sinning, that will convince Emma who is fifty-six to come to Christ and to leave that sin life of partying and sleeping with anybody who asks."

3. Brother Byron, seventy-seven and a retired pastor, moved to Houston from South Carolina to be near his family. He said he wants to continue to serve You by working with the church and in the Vintage group.

4. Brother Elmer is sixty-seven and married. His wife of forty years has early dementia and is in the memory-care section of the apartments. He said, "Pastor, will y'all pray for my wife and me. It's just us. We don't have any children and all our family is gone. I am thankful to be in a caring church like this. Since I came here, everybody has treated me like family. One of the young men, his name is Donald, he calls me Pops and comes to help me every Sunday get to a seat. He asked me to come fishing with him. I'm going to!"

5. Brother George is fifty-five and still working. He is divorced and a father to two boys, who live with their mother and her new husband. He said, "Pastor and First Lady, I am glad that I don't have drama with her and her husband over the boys. You know it is time

that I changed my ways and become a better father to my sons. Their stepfather, Dan, is active in his church and has gotten them involved. About a month ago, my oldest who is thirteen asked me if I was saved. Pastor, I stopped him when he was telling me about sin. After going to your church meeting here at the apartments, I have since apologized to him. He started telling me about the Gospel Project at the church he attends with his stepfather. I also called Dan and thanked him for giving the gospel to my boys and their mom."

6. Sister Pat is seventy. "Pastor and First Lady, this is sometin' else! All the time I have been going to churches—and I hate to say there's been several of them in my life—I have never had the pastor and his First Lady to come see me! This is sometin' else! Pastor, listen: just for the record my friends call me Pistol Packin' Pat. I have been licensed to carry this gun and I treat *Sam*—that's my gun's name—like my American Express card. I never leave home without it!" She was so excited to show us the gun and tell us that she is licensed to carry at her age. Lord, you know we asked her not to bring the gun to church.

7. Sister Mattie Mae is seventy-four, a retired schoolteacher and past church musician who played the organ in her church for forty years. She moved from Houston's north side to the southwest side to be near her daughter, who lives near the Seniors 50+ complex. "Pastor and First Lady Swan, I am glad to be at this GTJBC. Those were very mannerable young men who came to meet with us. Pastor, if you need a musician from time to time, I can still play, and my friend Annie Mae can still sing." She pointed with a flourish: "This is my organ.

"I know you both plan to see her next since she lives next door. We have been friends forever. She moved to be near me and my daughter. She is my daughter's godmother. All Annie Mae's family are gone. So, we take care of her."

8. Sister Annie Mae is seventy-three, Sister Mattie Mae's friend, and a retired school cook. "I moved here because I liked the apartments and wanted to 'live nicely like Mattie.' Did Mattie tell y'all I sang in the choir where Sister Mattie played the organ? She is good, and we will do praise and worship music anytime you need us. We still practice every Thursday in Mattie's apartment. Did you see that pretty organ she has over there? She has had that thing for years."

9. Sister Emma is single, fifty-six years old, and has been a nurse for the past twenty-seven years. She plans to retire in three years. She said, "Pastor Swan, I am like so many who grew up in the church, was baptized at eleven years old, but was never given the gospel until your group came. Thank you for sending the Elders to meet with us. I know my spiritual gift that I plan to use in the church's health ministry."

10. Sister Dianne is sixty-six and a mother of two adult daughters. One lives in Houston and the other in Katy. Sister Dianne works for the City of Houston. "Pastor and First Lady, I have the gift of working with children, so I look forward to serving in that ministry."

Pastor Swan ended his prayer, "And thank you again, Lord, for these sheep."

He returned to reading *Every Christian a Counselor.*

The Third Sunday

P astor Swan was ending his sermon on how to be "F. A.T.: Faith Available and Teachable in the Church."

"Before I close this morning, I want to introduce you to GTJBC's newest members. They all completed assimilation! First Lady Swan and I had a delightful home visit with each of them. When I call each of you by name, please come up here to get your shirt and assimilation completion certificate. Make sure you wear the shirts to GTJBC dedicated events. You members who have not met our newest members, please welcome your brothers and sisters with a Holy Hug after church services."

Pastor Swan then said, "Brother John, where are you?"

Brother John, sitting in the middle section of the church, stood up, waved his sermon notes, and yelled, "Oh Lordy! Pastor, here I am back here."

"Come on up front so your church family can see you!" The congregation clapped.

Pastor Swan said, "Brother Jimmy, wherever you are, follow Brother John."

Brother Jimmy said, "Look over here to your left, Pastor. I am here and coming." The congregation laughed and clapped.

Pastor Byron was sitting on the end of the third row behind the Elders.

"Pastor Byron, come join us. Church, Pastor Byron is a retired pastor and . . ." Before he could finish his sentence, everyone in the pews stood and applauded.

Pastor Swan smiled and hugged Pastor Byron. "Pastor Byron plans to get busy serving other Seniors in the church."

Pastor Byron waved and smiled as he got another round of applause.

"Brother Elmer, come on down and take your place on 'The Price Is Right'!"

The congregation laughed and clapped.

Brother Elmer was sitting next to Brother Donald, who stood up and said, "Come on, Pops; I'll walk with you." Brother Elmer smiled and held onto Brother Donald's arm so he could more easily get up from the pew.

"Brother George, are you in the house?" asked Pastor Swan.

"You better believe I am here and getting FAT like you've been preaching!" yelled Brother George. That brought more laughter and applause from the congregation.

"Church, I saved the best for last: our newest sisters! Let me introduce two who have been lifelong friends, Sisters Mattie Mae and Annie Mae! Wait before you start clapping; there is more to say about them. Sister Mattie Mae plays the organ and Sister Annie Mae sings. Sister Annie Mae said they have made 'Oh How Precious' their best song."

While the pastor introduced the sisters, they were walking side by side, smiling and waving with their hands in the air to the congregation like they were in a parade, while everyone clapped.

"Sister Dianne, let us see your face!" Pastor Swan announced. As the congregation clapped for her, Sister Dianne smiled and walked down the aisle from the left side of the church to join the others down front.

"Nurse Emma, where are you? We have another healthcare provider in our church!"

Applause and many "Amens!" were heard until Nurse Emma reached the group.

"Last but not least, I want you all to meet Sister Pat, who told me she would always have my back!"

Everyone laughed when the pastor turned his back to them.

"Sister Pat, where are you?"

Sister Pat sat on the right side of the church and began digging in her huge black purse that resembled a duffle bag.

Sister Pat shouted, "Wait, Pastor, just a minute! I got to make sure I show folk how I got your back!"

Sister Pat finally got up with her gun in her hand.

"That's a real gun?" asked the wide-eyed lady sitting next to Sister Pat.

Sister Pat held the gun above her head and said, "Yes, this gun is real, and I meant every word I said. I got the pastor's back, and don't nobody go messin' with him or the First Lady! My name ain't Pistol Packin' Pat for nothing!"

Sister Pat accidentally pulled the trigger, the gun fired, and a bullet hit a ceiling light. It sounded like a bomb exploding when it crashed to the tile floor.

With screams and yells to "hit the deck," people fell on the floor, crawling over each other and scrambling in every direction to get outside.

Sister Pat looked up in shock at the gun in her hand and fainted.

The gun fell from her hand and landed on her stomach.

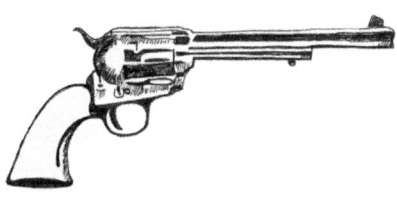

The Third Sunday, Part 2

At every church event and on Sundays, Going To Jesus Bible Church has two security guards who also work as fulltime constables in Fort Bend. Constables Ronald Harris and Larry Leonard were on duty that notable Sunday at the church.

They were walking their rounds and patrolling on the street side of the church when Constable Harris stopped abruptly. "Larry, did you hear a gunshot?"

Constable Leonard stopped, turned toward the church, listened for a second, and said, "Nope!"

Both started walking toward the building when members poured out of the church doors toward the parking lot, yelling and screaming, "Hurry, hurry up! Run, run faster!"

Constable Harris grabbed the arm of one member who was wearing an usher uniform and about to bolt past them. "Wait, what's going on?"

Before the usher could answer, Mary, a greeter, shouted, "Come quick! Somebody is shooting at the pastor!"

"What, for what?" Constable Harris asked.

"We don't know!" Mary squealed.

Constables Harris and Leonard started running toward the church, zig-zagging their way through people sprinting to their cars.

The Fort Bend Police and Fire Dept. paramedics, sirens blaring, were pulling up when the constables reached the church entrance.

"Everybody leave the building now!" commanded Constable Harris—his gun drawn and pointed upward.

"Which way did the gunman go after he shot the pastor?" Constable Leonard yelled at Elder Smith as he drew his gun from his holster.

Elder Smith motioned cautiously. "Leonard, put your gun away. Nobody shot him!"

Police Officer Charles from Fort Bend interrupted Elder Smith: "Sir, we got a call that someone shot at Pastor Swan, and he is down!"

Waving the paramedics into the sanctuary, Officer Charles followed them, along with the constables.

The paramedics were saying in unison, "Excuse us please! Let us pass! Excuse us!"

One paramedic yelled to the people still in the sanctuary, "Where is the pastor laying? Please move so we can get to him!"

A few people had circled, everyone gazing down at the floor.

When some moved back, the paramedics, constables, and Officer Charles (who had rushed in with gun drawn) skidded to a stop. Pistol Packin' Pat was still lying unconscious with her gun on her stomach.

"Where is Pastor Swan laying?" a paramedic panted, out of breath.

"Where's the guy who shot the pastor?" yelled Constable Leonard.

"Nowhere! Nobody was shooting at me," Pastor Swan answered calmly.

Constables Harris and Leonard and Officer Charles jumped at hearing Pastor Swan's voice. They peered at him for any visible blood, paused for a long moment, and then re-holstered their guns.

Constable Leonard said slowly, "Who shot at you?"

"Nobody," Pastor Swan replied quietly and pointed at Sister Pat. She was groggy but beginning to awaken on the gurney where the paramedics had placed her.

The pastor explained, "Sister Pat's gun accidentally went off while she was coming to the pulpit to show it."

Officer Charles questioned with growing irritation, "Why on earth was she trying to show off her gun in church?"

Pastor Swan smiled, "Officer Charles, this is such a long story, and I will not be pressing charges against her."

The officer snapped, "I will charge her if she does not have a permit to have this gun," and he removed the gun off her stomach.

"Oh, she has a permit," the pastor replied, now grinning broadly.

Sister Pat, more fully awake and looking confused at the people surrounding her: "Whuh happened? What's going on? Get me off this thing!"

One paramedic explained in an official voice, "You fainted, and we need to carry you to the hospital to get checked."

"Fainted! I never faint!" Sister Pat scoffed.

"Well, you did after you shot your gun and blew out that lamp," Elder Smith said pointedly as he motioned up to the blown-out light.

"What? I did that!?" Sister Pat gasped.

"Yep, and cleared out the church too, Pistol Packin' Pat!" Elder Smith said and started chuckling. Others in the group began laughing with relief and bemusement.

"Oh, my goodness! Did anybody get hurt? Where is Pastor Swan?" Sister Pat asked.

"I am right here, Sister Pat."

"Pastor, I am so sorry." Sister Pat tried to reach for the pastor's hand, and her handbag fell off the gurney and hit the floor. A small black-handled derringer slid out of the bag.

Everyone looked at the gun on the floor, stopped laughing, and like a choreographed dance, turned in unison to look at Sister Pat. She had covered her face with both her hands.

Twelve Church Ladies and the Church Van

The radio station rang out from the Fellowship Hall of Going To Jesus Bible Church. "Good Saturday morning! The time is 7:00 a.m.! Today will be a cool fall day here in Sugar Land. Expect a high of only 57 today for most of the area. Keep those jackets close by."

Elder Jones placed his black jacket on the round table by the Fellowship Hall's front door. Holding his Bible under his right arm, he jingled the van keys with his left hand while walking out to the van. Twelve women, members from Going To Jesus Bible Church, had gathered there. They waited for him to bring the van keys and to pray before they went on a day of shopping fellowship.

The van driver, Sister Martha, smiled and extended her hand where he dropped the keys. "Good morning, Elder."

"Good morning, ladies. I hope y'all have an enjoyable time today. I checked the van earlier and everything looks good. Sister Martha, please drive carefully."

"Elder, you know I drive a school bus every day for a living." Sister Martha smiled and pointed to the van: "I got this!"

Elder Jones nodded and said, "All right, ladies; let's pray."

Everybody got into a circle, held hands, and bowed their heads, before Elder Jones started the prayer.

"Dear Lord, thank You for this day. We praise and adore You, Father. We acknowledge we are sinners and in the Name of Your Son Jesus, please forgive us. Father, twelve members from this church are about to go on a fellowship shopping outing. Please keep them covered under your protection en route to the outlet mall, while shopping, and on their way back. In the Name of Your Son Jesus."

"Thank you, Elder. We appreciate your coming to see us off," said Sister Barbara as she stepped into the van with his help.

"Yeah, Brother Jones. Thank you." Sister Elvia put her right hand on the Elder's shoulder and grabbed the van door handle to step into the bus. She then sat down behind the driver's seat.

Sister Martha settled behind the wheel: "Let's get moving, ladies. Elder, on behalf of us all, we thank you."

Elder Jones helped the rest of the ladies get on the van. He waved, "Bye ladies, and be safe."

As soon as the van pulled onto Interstate 59/69 in Sugar Land headed north, Sister Elvia, who sat behind the driver, leaned forward and said, "Sister Martha, we do have the van until around 9 tonight, right?"

"Yep! Why do you ask, Elvia?"

"Well, a few of us were talking about not going to shop but instead to the casino up in Livingston. It's early. We have time to get there and back. We can stop by Walmart and pick up a few items to say we've been shopping."

Sister Martha said, "No ma'am, that is not a clever idea. We will be lying by doing that, and I will get into serious trouble with Pastor Swan."

Sister Elvia stood up. "Hey ladies, let's vote about going down 45 to the shopping outlets or staying on 59 to go to Naskila Casino!"

"Sister Elvia?"

"Yes, Sister Tammy?"

"Did the pastor give us permission to use the van to go gamble?"

"No, Tammy. Who is going to tell him?"

"Well, I do not think we should be going to that casino!" Sister Tammy responded with a piercing stare into Sister Elvia's eyes.

"Tammy, if we decide to go, you can shop at the casino shops! All in favor of going to the casino, hold up your hands!

Everybody but Sister Tammy and the driver held up their hands.

Sister Elvia grinned with triumph, clapped her hands together, and yelled, "The majority say go to the casino! Sister Martha, there are casino shops. We can shop there!"

Sister Martha did not answer but drove silently up I-59/69. When she got to the fork in the road, she took the 59 route. Everybody but Sister Tammy clapped and yelled.

Sister Elvia tapped Sister Martha on her shoulder and said, "God bless ya, and thank you, girl!"

Sister Martha gripped the steering wheel tightly and replied grimly, "I better not hear one word about this!"

"You won't and the pastor won't either! Right, Tammy?" yelled Sister Portia from the back of the van.

Sister Tammy refused to lift her eyes from reading the devotional book she had brought along for the ride.

After arriving at the casino, Sister Martha announced, "I am pulling out at 6:30 p.m. so don't be late. I promise I will leave you behind."

Sister Tammy waited for everyone to leave the van. She went to Sister Martha, who was still sitting in the driver's seat, and said sternly, "You know better and ought to be ashamed. I am going to sit in the restaurant until y'all finish wasting my God-given time and His given money."

After a full day, all the ladies were sitting in the van by 6:30 p.m.

17

and chatting about wins and losses. However, Sister Tammy refused to talk to anyone. Sister Martha tried to crank the van. The engine made a sound like a loud coffee grinder but would not start.

"Oh God no!!" moaned Sister Martha.

"What is it?" Sister Portia shouted from the last seat in the van.

"Use your head and guess!" Sister Tammy responded angrily.

Sister Martha pounded the steering wheel. "The van will not start!"

"What?!" yelled Sister Betty, interrupted from counting the 300 dimes she won from the slot machine.

"What do we do now?" muttered Sister Portia.

Sister Elvia replied sadly. "Unfortunately, Sister Martha's gotta call Elder Jones, since he is over van transportation."

Sister Martha sighed, "Now we are in deep trouble!"

Sister Tammy looked up from her devotional reading. "We? You mean you and them behind me. I was y'all's hostage!" She returned to reading.

Sister Martha ignored Sister Tammy and picked up her iPhone from the van's dash and placed the call on speaker. "Hey Siri, call Elder Jones."

"Hello, this is J. Jones. I cannot answer your call. If you want to reserve the van, speak with me on Sunday. If you are having van trouble, please call Pastor Swan at 832-777-7777. Have a blessed day!"

Sister Martha stared at the phone and then slowly turned around, peering at the van passengers who also heard Elder Jones's message.

They all looked shocked and even horrified, except for Sister Tammy. She continued to read her devotional.

The Sistahs

Carol, Dell, and Edna have been friends since high school. Their husbands are deceased.

Carol's only son lives in Dallas with his wife and two children. Dell does not have any children.

Edna has four children: James, John, Jennifer, and Jilda, who live in Houston. Edna's children treat Carol and Dell as if they were blood relatives. They call and visit "Aunt Carol" and "Aunt Dell" every week like they call and visit their mom.

Carol, Dell, and Edna live next to each other at #102, #103, and #104 in the Going To Jesus Bible Church's newly built Retirement/Senior Apartment Complex.

If there is not a church event or a personal social event, the trio has a weekly cooking, eating fellowship, and wine-sipping date after church. These get-togethers rotate among the three homes.

One recent Sunday, Dell hosted the Sistahs' dinner, featuring spaghetti, garlic bread, salad, and Chianti.

Carol brought the spaghetti and Dell furnished the salad. Edna, the garlic bread preparer, also served as the wine steward and poured the dinner prep wine into red wine glasses.

Edna held up her glass. "Before I bring in the garlic bread, I want to make a toast." Carol and Dell touched their glasses to Edna's.

Edna began, "First, Lord, thank You for my dear friends, my Sistahs. Sistahs, I thank God for you two. You have been my 'ride till we die' friends for fifty-plus good years. Most people can't say that! We can! God bless you both, and I love you with all my heart!"

Carol and Dell replied, "Hear! Hear!" They sipped the wine, nodded their heads at each other, and smiled.

Carol held out her hand toward Edna. "Please pass that bottle of wine to me. I better get wine for this spaghetti sauce before we kill this bottle."

Edna laughed, handed Carol the bottle of wine with her right hand, and then pulled another bottle of Chianti from her bag with her left hand. She held the bottle above her head. "No ma'am, Sistah Carol, we will not run out of this Chianti today."

Chuckling, they touched their glasses together and in unison said, "Hear! Hear!"

After a few minutes of enjoying the meal and planning a tea event for the church, Dell said, "Okay, enough tea planning. It's gossip time!"

With a tsk tsk, Edna replied, "Dell, gossiping is sinful. How often do you have to hear that from Pastor Swan?"

Carol smiled and sipped her wine. "Now, my Sistah, let's state only facts about a matter, which is not gossiping. Then we will not be sinning!"

Dell laughed and took a sip, "Heifer, call it what you want!"

Carol quipped, "I am going to call the pastor and tell him you need church discipline for gossiping and drinking."

They all giggled.

"Well, now to use proper terms. What facts do we need to know this week about our church folk?" Dell asked.

"You be too cute, missy," Carol smiled.

Edna poured wine into her glass and tilted the bottle toward Dell and Carol. They both shook their heads. "Well, the church is buzzing about the shopping crew who did not go shopping but went to the casino! I heard the van broke down and they had to call Pastor Swan to come help them."

"What!" Carol grinned. "Edna, you are lying. I have not heard that!"

Dell took her last sip of wine and held her glass out to Edna for more. "Nope! She is not lying. I saw them!"

Carol and Edna looked at each other and then at Dell.

Carol exclaimed, both surprise and doubt in her voice, "You saw them? You were at the casino?"

"Yep, I was there with my Cousin Ann. Y'all, when I saw the church bus turn into the driveway and park at the entrance, I was in the gift shop getting gum before we left to come back to Houston. I was in shock and moved to the window to see who was getting off the bus. I took out my cell phone and took their pictures as they got off the bus one by one. To be honest I thought it was Pastor Swan and the Elders pulling up, and I was waiting to get their picture!"

"Dell, you need to look at your heart. We are going to pray for you, thinking that way about our leaders!" Carol said as she laughed and took another sip.

"Girl, please. I do not care about the pastor and his posse having a little casino fun!" Dell huffed and then grinned, picking up her cell phone from the table. "Anyway, here they are. All twelve of them!" Dell scrolled through the photos for Carol and Edna to see.

Edna laughed until she could barely choke out the words: "Girl, you didn't speak to them?"

"Nope! I waited for all of them to leave the bus, and we scooted out the gift shop door after the driver parked and came into the casino! I can't remember her name, but here is the driver." Dell held up her phone and pointed to the picture. "Look, let me make it clear: I did

not speak 'cause I as a good Christian sister did not want to be respon-
sible for someone to fall by seeing me there at the casino!"

Carol poured another glass of wine, sighed, and said somberly, "I
am going to pray triple for your tail tonight! What were your plans for
taking pics of each of them?"

Dell took a sip of wine and replied, with as straight a face as she
could muster, "To have as my 'show and tell' for our dinner today!"

The Sistahs laughed until tears flowed down their cheeks.

"Dell, you are crazy! You also need prayer and church discipline!"
Edna retorted. They were all still wiping tears from their faces while
nodding their heads—even Dell.

GTJBC
Cell Fellowship Gathering

Going To Jesus Bible Church divided the church into community cells to keep members engaged and involved, plus to aid in consistent communication among the church members. A church deacon led each cell.

Deacon Moore had a fellowship meeting with his cell group of twenty-five at Sweet Tomatoes in Stafford. He and his wife Sylvia arrived first to make sure the reservations were in order.

GTJBC members Edna and Carol were the first cell members to arrive at the restaurant. Sylvia waved them toward the reserved tables when she saw them walking in. "Hi, ladies, what's going on?" She smiled and hugged each one. "Come sit next to me."

Edna grinned, sat on Sylvia's right, and responded, "Thanks."

Carol smiled and said, "Hi, Deacon." She then sat on Sylvia's left.

Sylvia glanced at Carol and Edna and began smiling, "Where is Dell, your triplet?" Everybody in the church knew the close friendship Carol, Edna, and Dell had. They had shared their sisterhood status with everyone.

Carol said, "Dell is coming later with Kathy. They are at the church's health-fair planning meeting."

"Oh My Goodness!" Sylvia started laughing.

Deacon Moore joined Sylvia in laughing, as did Carol and Edna. No one said a word. Their laughing did the talking for them. As patrons walked by their table, they smiled at the laughing group.

Deacon Moore wiped the tears from his eyes and commented, "Poor Doc and the rest of the planning committee." Sylvia, Carol, and Edna nodded in agreement while still chuckling.

None of them noticed that Dell and Kathy had arrived and walked up to the table. The laughter started sputtering when they heard Dell say, "Who told a joke?"

Edna replied, "Speaking of the devils!"

"Were y'all talking about us?" Kathy asked with a smile that didn't quite reach her eyes.

Deacon Moore nodded, still speechless.

Dell replied, "Who said what, who started gossiping about us, and who do we need to report to Pastor Swan to start church discipline?"

Deacon Moore got himself together and cleared his throat. "Sister, we did not need to say anything after Carol told us you and Kathy were serving on the health-fair committee together at the church." He couldn't contain himself and started laughing again.

Dell turned to Kathy, "I am not sure I get the meaning of that comment, do you?"

Kathy smiled, "No, but they better tell us."

Carol replied, "The two of you already know why we are laughing. Y'all know how y'all can be when you two are together in a meeting. So, sit down and tell us what y'all did to upset the meeting before the rest of the cell members arrive."

Kathy looked at Dell and started snickering.

Edna pointed at Dell but spoke to Kathy, "What did Dell do to create drama in the meeting?"

Dell looked at Kathy and held her finger over her mouth. "Hush, Kathy, they are being messy!"

Deacon Moore commented, "The four of us knew there would be some carryings-on because the dynamic duo planners were together on the committee!"

"Deacon Larry Moore, I am reporting you to the pastor," Dell said with a grin.

"Just tell us what the two of you did to upset the meeting!" Deacon Moore said, tears still rolling down his face. Sylvia handed her husband more tissues.

Dell gave an *I give up* shrug. "All right, all right. I confess I made a few comments to make a title change in one specific workshop. You see, one committee member invited Dr. Nathan Stark from Methodist Hospital to come to discuss prostate health. His workshop's title: 'How to Cope with Your Prostate Problems.'"

Kathy held up her hand and interrupted Dell. "Then our friend Dell said, 'Pastor, I don't have a prostate, but if I did, with that title I would not go to that workshop. It's like announcing to the church about my prostate problem.'

"Then she stood up and addressed the group: 'Who in here has a prostate problem that you need to deal with?' Y'all, Pastor Swan stood up quickly and made a *Time Out* sign before anyone started answering her."

The cell group again exploded with laughter.

Dell asserted, "Y'all know I was telling the truth about that workshop title."

Deacon Moore choked out the question, "What did Doc say?"

Kathy quickly responded, "Pastor Swan said, 'There is no need for anyone to answer Sister Dell. Sister, thank you; your point is well taken.'"

Deacon Moore, still wiping his eyes, asked, "I just want to know, did they change the title?"

Dell announced, "Pastor Swan knew what I was talking about! You better believe the workshop title was changed to **For Men Only: Taking Care of Your Health and Health Concerns.**"

Sister Hazel and COVID

Since the storm of COVID-19 mandates, sicknesses, and deaths, Pastor Swan placed all Going To Jesus Bible Church events on Zoom. Pastor Swan met with the church's cell-community group leaders to discuss Communion distribution plans for the next three months. The church traditionally served Communion on the first Sunday of each month.

Each community leader was assigned to call the church members in his group to give instructions on the dates and times to come to the church to collect their Communion supplies and masks the church had secured for the members. The pastor made sure the pickup times were staggered and followed the COVID-19 personal protection and distancing guidelines.

During the Zoom meeting, Elder Smith said, "Pastor Swan, you know I have Sister Hazel and Sister Betty on my list. Those two can be a handful to talk to. They've always got an opinion about everything. Can you get the First Lady to call them?"

The other team members laughed. Pastor Swan tried to control his voice by coughing. "Elder Smith, listen brother: all you need to do is tell them what, when, where. If they try to discuss or question anything beyond that, tell them to call me, okay?"

Shaking his head, Elder Smith replied, "If you say so, Pastor. But you know how they can be."

Pastor Swan placed his hand to the monitor to give Elder Smith a virtual touch on his shoulder. He smiled, "Elder Smith, you will be all right."

THE CALL DAY

"Lord, Hazel Lou is the next person on my list. Please keep me from going off on her. Help me to be loving and not end up with church discipline after dealing with this known fool.

"Sorry, Lord. Forgive me. I need not think of her like that. I know it takes one to know one. I have been trying to work on me not being a fool from time to time. Lord, in the Name of Jesus, please guide my lips and my heart when I talk to Hazel Lou. Amen."

He took a deep breath and dialed Sister Hazel's number.

"Hello, may I speak to Sister Hazel Lou?"

"Who's calling for Sister Hazel?" Sister Hazel asked in a soft, sexy voice.

"This is Elder Smith from the church."

Her soft voice climbed instantly to loud. "What do you want, Willie Smith!?"

"Sister Hazel, because we will not be back into the church building for the next three First Sundays, Pastor Swan has arranged for us to come to the church to pick up our Communion supplies for those Sundays. You will also get a mask for your future use when you come to get your Communion supplies on Saturday at 2:00 p.m. Make sure to wear your mask and gloves when you come next Saturday. And remember, your assigned pickup time is from 2:00–3:00 p.m."

Silence.

"Sister Hazel, are you there? Can you hear me?"

The silence continued.

"Sister Hazel, did you hear all I said? Are you there?"

"Willie, I am not deaf or dumb, and yes, I heard you!" she yelled into the phone. Even more loudly: "Willie, that disease is still out there killing us. Too many people don't wear masks and gloves. I do not plan to come out for Communion supplies. I have my own that I will use when it is time for Communion during the sermon on Sunday. Tell the pastor I love him and respect his leadership, but I just can't do it.

"I do not see the Communion supplies as essential because I can use my own. I have a pack of soda crackers and Nehi grape soda. I can break off a piece of soda cracker to eat and sip a little from my grape Nehi when it is time to drink. I am not taking extra risks by coming out to get stuff.

"Y'all know there will be some fools who will not be coming in masks and gloves to the church 'cause they want freedom and are refusing to do what is right according to the ordinance! Willie, I am telling you, I know the Lord will bless the piece of soda cracker that I break off and my grape soda that I will sip. Bye, Willie!"

Sister Hazel Lou then hung up.

THE CALL BACK

"Lord, please give me strength and guidance. I must call her back to clear up some things with her," Elder Smith prayed, dialing Sister Hazel's number again.

Sister Hazel's phone rang. She looked at the Caller ID and saw the number from Elder Smith. She yelled into the phone, "What do you want now, Willie?!"

Elder Smith spoke sternly and lovingly. "Sister Hazel Lou, please do not spread your opinions about the church's plans concerning distribution of Communion supplies or your Communion intentions and plans. Your opinion and intentions can lead to conflict and confusion in our church for baby and carnal Christians. If you insist on spreading your opinion and your Communion plans with others in the church, Sister Hazel, I insist that you talk to one of the biblical counselors at the church. First, seek counsel about having a troubled heart that is unloving. And second, explore the reasons you are acting like a carnal Christian. God bless you, and good-bye, Sister Hazel Lou."

Elder Smith hung up his phone.

'Til Baby Do Us Part

Myia had difficulty looking at Pastor Swan, who sat in the black leather rocker peering intensely at her. She sat on the black leather sofa facing him. Her eyes wandered back and forth from his eyes to his white collar, to the gold cross that hung around his neck, to her own folded wet hands clenched in her lap. She tried to rub her hands dry but then noticed how they left a sweaty spot on her blue silk dress.

Pastor Swan gently took her sweaty hands in his huge brown hands. He wiped the sweat from her hands onto the leg of his jeans. Then he stood and picked up the tissue box from his desk.

Wiping her left hand dry, he began speaking to her quietly. "Myia, you will have to tell Marcus. I cannot and will not support you in keeping this information from him."

Pastor Swan then tossed the wet tissue into the wastebasket and plucked a few more tissues from the box. "Myia, listen: Marcus is going to find out more, sooner rather than later."

Pastor Swan placed the tissues on the arm of his rocker, clasped both her hands, and began speaking in a fatherly tone. "Myia, first let's pray for God's forgiveness, wisdom, and direction to share this information with Marcus."

Myia snatched her hands away and began crying. "Pastor Swan, Marcus will leave me. I will just die if he leaves me!"

"Myia, you are pregnant by Marcus's brother. I know Marco died in a car wreck three weeks ago, but there is not and will not be a suitable time for sharing this information about your pregnancy. You cannot function as if this is Marcus's baby."

"But Pastor Swan, no one has to know. They are identical twins. The baby is going to look like both."

"Myia, please stop it! You had an adulterous relationship with your husband's brother. You know that is a sin. It is not about who needs to know or who the baby will look like. You have broken your marriage vows and you need to ask God and your husband for forgiveness."

"Pastor Swan, please! I can't tell him. I know he will leave me!"

Pastor Swan gave her another tissue to wipe her tears.

At that same time, Marcus was driving home from work. He turned into the entrance of the neighborhood where he and Myia lived in their apartment.

Stopping at the intersection, he looked to the left and noticed the Going To Jesus Bible Church. His wife's blue Camry sat in the parking lot. As he mulled over that sight, he saw the church's LED sign featuring a daily Bible verse: "Trust in the Lord with all your heart; do not lean on your own understanding."

Marcus smiled and began talking loudly to himself. "Pastor Swan, having this church here in the neighborhood has been a blessing. I see you have finally got Myia in, since she's a Hospital Administrator, to plan the upcoming health fair! Let me see how I can help."

Marcus pulled his blue Jeep Grand Cherokee next to his wife's Camry. "Poor Myia, get ready to oversee the health fair. My dear, Pastor Swan is determined to get us all healthy." Marcus smiled and thought about how his brother Marco used to trick the pastor into thinking he was Marcus. "I miss you, Marco! You were my main man."

Marcus walked toward the office reception area. Brenda, Pastor Swan's secretary, was walking out and greeted him. "Hi, Marcus. I need to run to the sanctuary. Have a seat, and I'll be right back to let them know you are here."

Marcus walked in and sat in the office chair for a moment. He muttered to himself, "She does not need to announce me." Marcus got up and headed toward the pastor's office, calling "Hello, hello?" He did not receive an answer.

He continued to stroll down the hall toward the pastor's office. Pastor Swan and Myia were so engaged in the conversation that neither heard Marcus. As Marcus reached Pastor Swan's office door, he heard Myia crying. He slowed his pace and stood outside the door, which was ajar, and listened.

Sobbing with her face in her hands, Myia said, "Pastor Swan, when I tell Marcus that I am pregnant with Marco's baby, will you help me? Does he really have to know about the baby? I cannot tell him. He will leave me. He does not have to know!"

Marcus caught his breath, tears filling his eyes.

Pastor Swan leaned forward, held Myia's hands, and calmly replied, "Listen, Myia: I will be there with you, but you have to tell Marcus."

Marcus slowly backed away from Pastor Swan's door and then walked quickly down the hall and out of the office area. He could not stop the tears streaming down his face. He sprinted toward his car.

Sitting in the Jeep crying, Marcus began shouting to himself and periodically slapping his car dashboard. "We have been married for two years! I don't believe what I just heard! She has been sleeping with my brother. Oh God no! And carrying his baby! 'Not tonight, Marcus.' 'Wait until the weekend, Marcus.' 'I am PMSing, Marcus.' 'It's too late.' 'I need to rest, I'm tired.'

"Hell to you, Marco! She is my wife, and you were my brother! Man, you died just weeks ago in an awful wreck. If you were here, I'd take you out today!"

Marcus looked at the Subway bag lying on the passenger seat and took out the napkins to wipe his eyes. It was Marcus's turn to pick up dinner. He had stopped at Subway to get sandwiches for Myia and himself.

He threw the sandwiches out of the car window and drove out of the parking lot, passing Brenda. She waved at him. He stared straight ahead and didn't respond.

Brenda entered the church office and headed toward Pastor Swan's office. She heard Myia and the pastor talking. She knocked on the half-open door. Pastor Swan said, "Come on in."

Brenda said, "Did y'all see Marcus? I just saw him drive away."

Myia looked stunned and replied, "What?! He was here?"

Marcus drove to his and Myia's apartment. He climbed the stairs and unlocked the door. Walked directly to his computer, he hit his mailbox icon, clicking the Health Link Clinics message from his friend Robert and replying.

Dear Robert,

I accept your offer for the CFO position.

Yep, I can start in four weeks.

I am finishing my contract work here in about a week and I can do that remotely.

I will see you in Atlanta later this week and look for an apartment.

I'm leaving Houston tonight to head home to Rome, Georgia, to hang out for a while with my cousins Jackie and Erica.

I will call you to get the frat bros together so we can party!

See ya, man,

Marcus

Marcus then hit the new message icon. He began typing on a blank document page to his wife.

Dear Myia,

I would like to speak with you, but I cannot at this time. If I open my mouth to you, it will be as Pastor Swan would put it: "open and very unloving!" So, I am writing to you instead. I could not put my finger on your relationship with Marco, but I knew there was something between the two of you. I guess my love and devotion to you were not enough. You had to have my brother, too. And now you have his child.

You know something, I forgive you and Marco at this very moment. But I will not stay married to you or raise your and Marco's child. Marco's recent death, finding out about you sleeping with him and your love child with him, is more than I want to take. You are right about me leaving you if I found out.

I love you; I forgive you, but I have left you.

Love to you and may God bless you and Marco's baby,

Marcus

He hit the Send button.

Myia was still sitting in Pastor Swan's office when her phone pinged, showing an incoming e-mail.

Marcus threw his clothes into two large suitcases, put the luggage in his jeep, and drove to I-59N. Then he exited to I-10E, heading to Georgia.

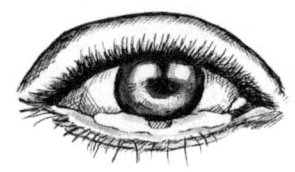

Ain't Happening

Marsha and Tisha had collapsed into their favorite soft chairs, feet up on ottomans, relaxing in their cozy apartment after tiring work days.

"Marsha, how was today?" Tisha asked her housemate.

"Girl, we are preparing for a JCAHO Survey at the hospital, and everybody is acting crazy!" Marsha replied, shaking her head. "We try to insist that each department stays ready, so we can prevent rushing around at the last minute. As you well know, there are always a few departments that will not follow instructions in the off-survey years and then start acting a fool when we are not at their beck and call to help them put documentation in place for the survey!

"And what about you? How was your day?" Marsha queried. "Hope it was better than mine!"

"Marsha, I must constantly remind my family members that my nursing job does not give me an Oprah's salary. Girl, today Auntie Emma called me, asking for money to get my cousin Johnson out of jail for stealing a video game. Mind you, this is the third time this boy—twenty-two years old!—has been locked up for stealing stupid crap like tennis shoes, jerseys, and mess like that. I have sent money to help her with that fool twice. I told her that my salary as an RN does not allow me to keep helping get people out of jail behind stupid decisions like stealing. Or to give money to family who desire something they cannot afford or want it because somebody else has it.

"This is the part of my talk with Auntie today that floored me most. I asked Auntie about my cousin, her other son Ashton. She said, 'Ashton is working two part-time jobs and staying in school at Highland College. Ashton is doing fine and does not need anything like Johnson does!'

"Then I said, 'Auntie, is there anybody helping Ashton buy books, gas, or anything to keep him going?' Girl, I wanted to go through that phone line to strangle her when Auntie Emma said this craziness to me: 'Look Tisha, Ashton is working and doing all right. But Johnson is locked up and needs our help. Life has been so hard on him. It's hard for Johnson to keep a job 'cause he has trouble getting up in the morning. Johnson is not a morning person. You know even when Johnson was little, he was not a morning person. It was hard getting Johnson up to go to school. Thank God, Johnson graduated from high school!'

"I then asked Auntie about Johnson's second-shift job at the mill in Calhoun. He would work 3-11, and that doesn't require him getting up in the morning.

"She said, 'Johnson did not get along with the supervisor.' According to Auntie Emma, Johnson said he did not like his supervisor 'telling him what to do rather than asking him to do a task.' Auntie went on to explain that Johnson told his supervisor, 'You ain't my daddy. You supposed to be asking me and not telling me!'

"My Auntie continued with 'Well, that got Johnson fired from the last job. Tisha, you know Johnson has always been sensitive and gets mad easily. That supervisor should have talked to Johnson like he was a grown man. I told Johnson he was right to expect to be respected and to take his time to find the right job.'

"Marsha, when my Auntie uttered those words, I tried to remember the sermon from Pastor Swan about how to be gentle, open, and loving when responding to foolishness. Although my first desire was to go slap her. I prayed and asked God for forgiveness and guidance before I went into my speech.

"Then I said, 'Auntie Emma, I want you to listen to me carefully. I am not using one cent of my hard-earned money to help get Johnson's sorry tail out of jail. He knows better than to steal. As many times as he has gotten caught, he should realize he is too stupid to steal. An occupation that does not include stealing is his smart set.'

"'Anyway, Auntie, my days are over of investing in my brothers and sisters who continue to attempt to make crime a career. They intentionally avoid a 9-5 job, because dependence on family for support is successful to keep them going. Hear me well, Auntie: from this day forward, I plan to invest whatever dollars I can spare into family and a few friends who will give me a positive return on my investment. For too many years too many of us have lost property, homes, and hard-earned money by repeatedly financing family members who want attorneys, money on the jail books, and cigarettes, because they insist on trying to get money and other nonsense stuff without working at whatever job they can get.'

"'I can count on one hand the families and friends who have made loans or sold their property to help those of us and others who needed help to finish college. But y'all just decided those going to jail for foolishness is a better investment. However, if Johnson is wrongly jailed or is in for self-defense, I will do all I can for him. From this day forward, I am sending a message to family and friends: I will not ignore you if your path is with intentions of doing and struggling for what is right and productive. Auntie, just think about it. How much have family and friends lost by financing folk who have had no intentions of doing right, while those who tried to do right by going to school or working whatever jobs to make ends meet have gotten ignored by family and friends?'

"'Auntie, please text me Ashton's telephone number. Thanks, I just got it. I need to see how I can help him this month. I will pray for Johnson, but money from me for him *ain't happening!* God bless you, Auntie. I love and will see you later.'

"Marsha, I hung up the telephone."

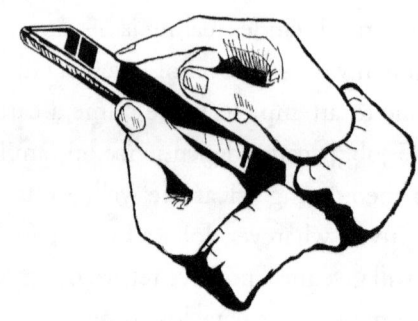

The Mess Ministry

Pastor Swan and First Lady Margaret Swan love spending time with Bridgett and Royce Taylor.

First Lady Margaret and Bridgett have been friends since elementary school. They went to the University of Houston and graduated together. Bridgett met Royce at the University.

Recently Pastor Swan and First Lady Margaret met with Bridgett and Royce at Local Foods to discuss plans for the church's marriage ministry and then to go to a movie together.

The pastor and his wife were sitting, sipping tea and talking in the Local Foods' outdoor patio when Margaret looked at her Apple watch. She told her husband, "Bridgett says she is here."

First Lady Swan spoke into her watch to reply, "We are sitting outside."

Bridgett opened the patio gate. Margaret waved to her and stood up to greet her with a hug.

Bridgett said, "What's up, girlfriend?" She gave Margaret a hug.

Bridgett then walked over to hug Pastor Swan, who was standing with a big grin and his arms open.

Pastor Swan held Bridgett's left ring finger and asked, "Where is my brother who is attached to this ring?"

"He is coming. Some issues arose at the school for Principal Royce to resolve. He texted that he will be here in about thirty minutes," Bridgett replied.

Pastor Swan let go of her finger and pulled out a chair for her.

"Thanks, Pastor," Bridgett sat down. "It feels good out here today. I'm glad you chose this spot, Margaret."

"You are welcome, my sistah!"

"What thoughts have you and Royce had about the marriage ministry?" Pastor Swan asked.

"Before I answer you, I want to share with you a ministry that has been weighing heavy on my heart," Bridgett announced with a mischievous smile.

Pastor Swan replied, "Okay, let's hear your thoughts."

Bridgett grabbed Pastor Swan's hand, looked him in the eyes, and said, "Pastor, I want to start a Mess Ministry!"

Pastor Swan started laughing, snatched his hand from her grasp, then tapped her wrist with his right hand. Then he looked at his wife and said, "Margaret, what are we going to do with her?"

"Girl, you are crazy!" First Lady Swan was laughing between coughs from choking on her tea.

"Pastor, a few days ago when we were cleaning the sanctuary, three church folk came up to ask if I had heard about 'the twin brothers in the church being married to the same woman and now she is having twins and does not know who the father is.' They went on to say one of the brothers killed his brother.

"I nipped that mess in the bud. I will not tell you all of what I said, because I was open and 'slightly' unloving 'a little bit.' I will tell you that I was polite when I told them (using air quotes) 'to stop gossiping and spreading lies. If our brothers and sisters have any issues, we need to help and not hinder each other by making up mess, containing mess, and carrying mess about each other.'

"Anyway, when we left from cleaning, they were not speaking to me. That is when I started thinking about the Mess Ministry."

Pastor Swan tried to speak between guffaws, but Bridgett held up her hands. "Wait, Pastor: give me one minute to finish my proposal. Based upon my recent experience with 'yo church folk' (using air quotes again), I can fill this ministry with three categories of members:

"**The Mess Creators** who start mess with gossip and outright lies.

"**The Mess Carriers** who enjoy spreading gossip by telling and asking as many people as possible about the gossip and lies.

"**The Mess Containers** who support and serve as the lie verifiers for the Mess Carriers."

Bridgett smacked the table, chuckled wryly, and asserted, "You know this ministry will work. Our church has the Mess Creators, the Mess Carriers, and the Mess Containers! I must admit that I had trouble finding this ministry discussed in the Bible. But I know you can give me some scriptures to support it, right?"

First Lady Margaret, still laughing, lay her head down on the table.

Bridgett retorted, "Why are you laughing, girl? You know the church is full of messy folk. We can put them all together, corral the mess, and then quickly nip the mess coming from them! I know we are laughing, but I am dead serious."

Wheezing and raising his right hand, Pastor Swan asked, "May I speak now, Sister Bridgett?"

"Yes, Pastor, go right ahead!" Bridgette waved her hand with a flourish while giving him permission to speak.

Smiling, the pastor replied, "Sister Bridgett, the answer is *no,* there are no scriptures to support the Mess Ministry and *no* to the Mess Ministry. Although I must admit the devil's hand will be all in that ministry and it will be extraordinarily successful, popular, and full of those we continue to help mature in God's Word, rather than the devil's deeds."

Pastor Swan, spotting Royce coming toward them, stood and welcomed Royce with a hug. "Hey man, how is it going?"

"All is well, Pastor." He leaned over, kissed Bridgett, and said, "Hi Baby." Then, "Hello, First Lady."

Royce took a seat next to Bridgett. "I saw y'all laughing. I know my wife was talking about . . ."

"The Mess Ministry," Pastor Swan completed Royce's sentence.

Royce nodded while chuckling, "Man, I have been cracking up over that and told her to put the Mess Ministry in her act on stage!"

Pastor Swan pointed to Royce and said, "Royce, rap it!"

Margaret and Bridgett turned in unison toward Royce, who started rhyming.

"Bridgett, the MM won't work in GTJBC today.
"There's nothing more you need to say!"

Royce then pointed to Pastor Swan, who added,

"The MM is a funny fleshy thought!
"But the Lord will slap us all if it's sought."

Margaret and Bridgett looked at each other and shrieked hysterically.

The Singing Duet

Every First and Third Sunday, Elder Plummer and Elder Douglas oversaw the Seniors' Sunday school meeting at Going To Jesus Bible Church, following the morning church service.

Pastor Swan allowed forty-five minutes between church service and Sunday school for stretching, snacking, and bathroom breaks.

To begin the Seniors' Sunday school, Elder Plummer announced, "Please take a seat, everyone. After I pray, Elder Douglas will play a song for us and then we will dive into our lesson.

"Dear Lord, thank You for today. Thank You for giving us another opportunity to praise You, to worship, and to learn more about You in this Sunday school. You, Father, have given us grace and more than we deserve. Forgive us for our sins and please open our hearts to hear and to embrace Your Word in this Sunday school lesson. In the Name of Jesus, we pray."

All twenty-five Seniors in the room responded, "Amen"!

Elder Douglas (a professional musician) carefully removed his beautiful white soprano saxophone from its black case.

He brought the sax up to his mouth and began to play "His Eye Is on the Sparrow."

Unexpectedly, Sister Margie suddenly rose from her seat, straightened her tightly fitting red skirt, and stood beside Elder Douglas.

She clasped her right hand with her left and placed her folded hands at her waist.

Sister Margie held her head back, closed her eyes, and began to sing along, her piercing voice squeaking in an off-key, operatic mezzo soprano quaver.

Several Sunday school members started glancing at each other, wincing at each sour note. Others looked too shocked to move, and a few quietly snickered as Sister Margie sang. Elder Douglas gave Sister Margie a double-take look but kept on playing.

When Elder Douglas finished the instrumental, Sister Margie was not ready to stop singing. Her finale was a squealing crescendo: "And IIIIIIIIIII knowoooooo He watchesssssssss meeeeeeeeeeee!" Sister Margie smiled, bowed, and walked back to her seat.

Some members of the group clapped uncertainly while others continued to snicker.

Elder Plummer walked slowly to the front of the room, turning toward Elder Douglas, "Brother, thank you. We love it when you play for us."

Elder Plummer peered seriously at Sister Margie. "Oh my, Sister, you killed that sparrow this morning!" He collapsed into his chair, raised one hand as if appealing to the Almighty, but then lowered his gaze to the floor.

If That's What You Want!

Ashley grew up as a "Daddy's girl," learning at an early age to read, swim, hunt, fish, play dominos, softball, checkers, and straight and bid whisk. She learned all about football but did not play—and drank whiskey, but rarely. She mastered every skill that John, her father, presented to her.

She developed a love for shooting guns. Her father taught her gun safety and took her weekly to the gun range on Bellaire to develop her shooting skills. A sharpshooter at thirteen, Ashley's shooting skills earned her admiration from the people who attended the gun range and watched her win trophies.

Ashley's mother, Pauline, often objected to her husband's teaching Ashley fishing and especially hunting. "You are making my and your only child and daughter, my princess, into a tomboy" were comments John heard often from Pauline.

He always retorted, "Pauline, my Honey Bunny, our Ashley is still our princess. She needs to know outdoor stuff plus games like your indoor cooking, cleaning, and creating: that 'girly' stuff. She is a better well-rounded princess."

After graduating from Bellaire High School, Ashley went to

Hampton University. After four years at Hampton, she went to Law School at Howard University. There Ashley met her husband, Marvin; he was attending the College of Architecture and Engineering.

Ashley and Marvin got married in December 2017 after graduating from their programs. They moved back to Houston following their honeymoon and joined Going To Jesus Bible Church in Sugar Land. Ashley worked in the children's ministry. Marvin was in the media team ministry.

In January 2018 Ashley accepted a position at a law firm in Sugar Land and was given the label of a "brilliant, tough cookie" by her attorney colleagues.

Marvin became a software engineer at a software company in Sugar Land. He partnered with Elanor, a single, bright, and attractive woman.

Marvin and Elanor gained the reputation as the go-to team for quick software development and problem-solving. Marvin gave Elanor the nickname "El" and the name caught on. They had the "ME" Team title among their section colleagues for their initials **Marvin** and "**El**."

After working together closely for a year, Marvin and Elanor's work intimacy moved into a romantic intimacy. When Ashley traveled away from home for work, Marvin would often invite "El" to his and Ashley's home.

While working in a private luncheon meeting one day, El looked at Marvin, who was staring at his laptop screen. "Marvin, will you stop for a minute? Let's talk about our situation."

His eyes still fixed on the laptop, Marvin muttered, "What about our situation? We are developing a plan for evaluating Group 2's software."

"Marvin, look at me for a minute, please," El insisted.

Marvin looked up and stared into her eyes. "Okay, what situation, El?"

"I am talking about us getting together! When are you going to tell Ashley about your plans to divorce her?"

"El, I will tell her soon."

"Marvin, you said that last month. I am ready for you to tell her now—or I will move on."

"El, where is this coming from?"

"Marvin, I am tired of sneaking around with you! It's now or never!" El folded her arms with a pout.

"All right, El; I will tell her tomorrow, Friday. Is that soon enough? Come here, please."

"What do you want, Marvin?"

"A smile and a kiss," Marvin answered.

"I'll give you a smile. I will kiss you after we tell her tomorrow. I am coming with you."

"Why, El? I got this!"

"Marvin, I want to make sure that you follow through. This is the third time you have promised to tell her and then changed your mind because 'it is not the right time.'" El crossed her arms even tighter.

"El, she is getting off early tomorrow. Telling her tomorrow will give her a few days to recover from the news before going to church and back to work. Speaking of church, I know I'll have issues with Pastor Swan and the Elders about my decision and our relationship."

"I will go with you to tell them, too," El snipped.

Marvin stared at her and then changed the subject. "Let's finish reviewing this data."

"Okay, but I am coming with you tomorrow!"

FRIDAY, 6:00 A.M.

Marvin got out of bed and walked into the bathroom. Ashley was already there, rinsing her mouth.

He gently rubbed Ashley's back and murmured, "Good morning."

Ashley turned on the water and spat the rinse into the sink. "Good morning. Do you want to meet me at Pappasito's after you get off work? Someone from Air Con is due here at noon. I pray he finishes repairing the air conditioner in a couple of hours."

Marvin's heart began to race. "No, El and I have a late meeting."

"On a Friday?" Ashley looked puzzled.

"Well, you know software engineering is not a 9-5 job!"

Ashley held up her hands, "Hold up, buddy. I didn't intend to ruffle your feathers. Sorry I asked you for a date. I will be leaving for work shortly. Have a super blessed day, my brother."

Ashley walked out of the bathroom, dressed, walked to the front door, and yelled, "I'm gone!" She made an effort not to slam the front door and then locked it.

FRIDAY, NOON

When Ashley got home at noon, the AC repairman was waiting for her.

FRIDAY, 3:00 P.M.

The repairman left after fixing the AC.

FRIDAY, 3:30 P.M.

Ashley called the Bellaire Shooting range to make a Saturday reservation. She then began making a "dagwood" sandwich.

Admiring her huge sandwich, she began muttering, "Subway, watch out! I can put you out of business with my sandwich-making skills! Y'all better be glad I like practicing law."

Ashley smiled, grabbed a kombucha and her sandwich, strolled into the den, and clicked on Sirius XM 66. George Howard's "Do I Ever Cross Your Mind" was playing. Ashley swayed with the music as she listened, ate, and enjoyed her favorite lemon-strawberry drink.

After eating, Ashley lay down on the sofa, drifting into sleep listening to "Light above the Trees" by Keiko Matsui.

FRIDAY, 5:00 P.M.

"My goodness, I took a good long nap!" Ashley moved the XM channel to Classic Soul 49. Frankie Beverly was crooning out "Joy and Pain."

"God, please let me have joy when my husband comes home and not pain. I am not feeling them the same today!" Ashley spoke loudly to herself.

"I Am Looking for a Love" by Bobby Womack came on next. Ashley got up, dancing into the guest bathroom.

Ashley heard the door chime. She yelled, "Marvin, I am in the bathroom. I'll be out in a minute."

Walking closely behind Marvin, El asked, "How did she know you're here?"

"El, the door chimed when we walked in. Didn't you hear it?"

"Where Is the Love" was playing on the radio when Ashley walked out. She looked startled to see El standing next to Marvin.

"Hi, Elanor, how are you?"

"I am simply fine, Ashley. How are you?"

"So far so good. I did not expect to see you today."

Ashley looked at Marvin. "You guys have a crisis to resolve?"

"We have a project to complete," Marvin answered solemnly.

"Okay, Mr. Sunshine. The office is nice and cool now. I will see y'all later," Ashley smiled and turned to walk toward the kitchen.

"Ashley, wait!" Marvin yelled, then jumped at the sound of his own voice.

"What is it, Marvin?" She stopped and turned around.

"Ashley, I'm divorcing you!" Marvin motioned to El to join him. "I am going to marry El."

El grabbed Marvin's hand and stared into Ashley's eyes.

Johnnie Taylor was singing "Everything Is Out in the Open" on the radio.

51

"What? What did you say?" Ashley looked directly at Marvin and ignored El.

"Ashley, I am leaving and divorcing you to marry El." Marvin held up El's hand.

"Elanor is El, now?" Ashley questioned.

"Yes, I call her El; that is what she is to ME. I am *M* for Marvin, and she is *E*, my El."

FRIDAY, 5:30 P.M.

Ashley looked at Marvin and Elanor and stated coolly, "No problem. If that is what you want." She then held up her right hand and said, "Please excuse me for a brief minute."

She turned and went into her office. Looking over her guns, she chose the .22 pistol with a pearl handle and tucked the gun into the back of her pants.

Ashley re-entered the living room, quickly pulled the gun from her pants, and aimed at Marvin and Elanor.

"Ashley, wait! I thought you said, 'No problem'!" Marvin yelled, dropping El's hand and holding up both his hands.

"Ashley, stop! Don't hurt me!" El squealed.

"Missy, you march into *my* house with *my* husband, eyeing me, and holding my husband's hand while he is talking about leaving me to marry you! Put yourself in my shoes. What would *you* do, little missy?"

"Ashley, what is with you?" Marvin, still holding up both his hands, stepped in front of El. "You said, 'No problem'!"

"Marvin, shut up! Both of you lie down on your stomachs!" Ashley spat out.

El turned to run out the front door.

Ashley shot a pillow on the sofa.

"Stop, Ashley, please!" El shouted, her voice shaking.

"Please stop!" Marvin begged.

"I have stopped for now! But I want you both to lie down on your stomachs!" Ashley commanded.

"Why?!" Marvin choked out.

Ashley shot another pillow. "I will make the next shot a person and not a pillow! Now both of you, face down!"

"Ashley, please don't do something you will regret!" Marvin shouted while he motioned to El to join him on the floor. He reached over to hold El's hand.

Ashley stepped over them and opened the front door.

"Ashley, what are you doing?" Marvin demanded.

Standing at the open door, Ashley used her left hand to beckon them toward the door. "I want the two of you to crawl out of this door like the snakes you are!"

"We are not crawling anywhere!" Marvin snarled.

Using her sharp-shooting skills, Ashley shot a bullet that landed between Marvin and El, thudding into the wood plank that separated them.

El and Marvin, holding their ears, gasped and then screamed with terror in unison, "Ashley, stop!!"

"I will stop when you two snakes crawl out of here. Marvin, you know I am good with a gun and can blow your brains out. Or maybe shoot something else off, right?"

"Ashley, are you going crazy?" Marvin yelled.

"Marvin, this is yours and El's last chance! Crawl now!" She aimed at his right knee.

"El, crawl with me, please. She is *really* good with a gun," Marvin begged, his voice trembling. He began crawling quietly, El sobbing and following him, toward Ashley, who stood solemnly at the front door.

Ashley yelled, "Stop!"

"We are crawling out, Ashley. What more do you want?" Fear choked Marvin's voice.

Stepping over Marvin and El at the threshold, Ashley quickly grabbed El's purse and Marvin's car keys from the floor, then threw them into the front yard.

Ashley began kicking Marvin's and El's legs. "God forbid, ME's items remain behind. Do not worry, Marvin: I will mail your possessions to your office. It is not in your best interests to return to this house! Now keep crawling, you snakes!"

El squealed and sobbed while crawling over the threshold.

Laughing and pointing at El, Ashley exclaimed, "Missy, why are you crying? You were so tough earlier when you were staring me down. I know you came here with this fool to make sure he tells me! You got what you wanted! This is what you want, right? I repeat, *you got it!*"

Marvin and El crawled successfully to the front porch, jumping up to bolt to his car.

Ashley said, "Later, snakes!" and slammed the front door. She picked up her cell phone and punched in numbers.

"Hello, Pastor Swan—this is Ashley Brooks. I need your assistance. I just threatened and shot at my husband and his lover El. They both came to the house and . . ."

The pastor interrupted: "Sister Ashley, are they injured or dead?"

Ashley paused, hearing a siren in the distance and knowing the police were likely speeding toward her house after her neighbors heard shots and surely called 9-1-1.

Both tears and laughter popped out as Ashley replied, "No, sir! They are not injured or dead. They are just *really* scared!"

A Messy Situation

hile constructing a gazebo for the marriage ministry's upcoming event in the Family Life Center of Going To Jesus Bible Church, Pastor Swan and Jerry enjoyed visiting. They did not notice Eva as she walked by, on her way to the restroom in the facility.

Eva made it a point to stay out of Pastor Swan's and Jerry's sight, so she could overhear their conversation about divorce.

"Pastor Swan, I see you do not agree with the divorce," Jerry reiterated loudly.

"Nope, I do not!" Pastor Swan reacted quickly.

"Come on, Doc! Why drag it out when the relationship is over? What is the point in suffering in an unwanted relationship? What if I hold off on the divorce for eight months?" Jerry responded.

Eva made stealthy ninja moves to get a little closer to listen to Jerry and the pastor.

"Nope, a biblical counseling program is in order," Pastor Swan retorted.

"Come on now: eight months!"

Eva forgot about her bladder needs and eased out of the Family Life Center. She found her cell phone to speed-dial her best bud, Jennifer.

"Yes ma'am, Sister Eva! What's up?" Jennifer cheerfully answered her phone.

"Girl, I just heard Jerry, the handsome one who sounds like Luther in the choir, tell Pastor Swan about his plans to divorce his wife Madeline in eight months!"

"What?!"

"Jennifer, I heard it with my own ears! I know Madeline from our Sunday school group. Somebody needs to tell her what's coming!" Eva spoke urgently.

"I say we wait to see how this unfolds. I want to know who he is divorcing her to be with! This can be some real 'tune in tomorrow' drama!" Jennifer hissed.

"Got it! Let's see who slipped up that handsome hunk!" Eva agrees to wait.

"Eva, I bet he is fooling around with somebody at the church. You know these men are too stupid to look outside their own church!"

"I am going to get some popcorn and Coke and watch this drama. Can you believe he told Pastor Swan outright about his plans to divorce poor Madeline in eight months! I should have waited to see who he said he is leaving her for!"

"Eva, that's what these low-down-dirty handsome men do! Use you up and then go to somebody else! Hey, when we see Madeline in Sunday school this Sunday, let's get her and pray for her and with her."

"Jennifer, that's a super idea. Let's go to Local Foods on Dunstan this Thursday after work. We will bring our husbands a late meal from there on Thursday. It will be just in time for them to enjoy the Thursday night football game. Dallas is playing somebody! Thursday is our early workday. I will pick you up around 4:30."

Meanwhile, back in the Family Life Center . . .

Pastor Swan shook his head. "Nope, Jerry, no divorce, but counseling!"

"Pastor, you know divorcing is the kind of mess that sells books. People love mess, love to see mess, and love to read about mess!" Jerry pointed out, laughing.

"Brother Jerry. My books sell and they are far from being loaded with carnal believer mess or secular mess!" Pastor Swan countered with a head nod and smile.

Jerry's cell phone rang. He held up his left hand to the pastor. "Just a sec, Doc, this is Madeline. Hey Babe! Pastor and I will finish our tasks in about five, ten minutes."

Jerry paused to listen to Madeline and touched Pastor Swan on the shoulder. "Doc, the Loves of our Lives say we are too slow. They finished their assignments thirty minutes ago."

Jerry spoke loudly while chuckling into the cell: "Sister Madeline and First Lady Swan, Pastor and I are happy that you guys finished your assigned tasks 'thirty minutes ago' and we apologize for being 'slow' as you both described us. However, we are *sure!*"

Laughing, Pastor Swan gave a thumbs-down signal.

Jerry added, "Doc is sending the thumbs down to you both! Babe, wait a minute before you hang up! Our beloved pastor highly suggests that I do not let the characters in my book get a divorce but rather go to biblical counseling. I told him mess sells books."

Pastor Swan pulled Jerry's right hand toward him and spoke into the phone, "Sister, I informed your husband that my books sell, and secular mess is not in them!" Pastor Swan then pushed the cell phone back to Jerry's mouth.

"I give up! I'll send the characters to biblical counseling! We will see y'all in about fifteen." He returned the cell phone to his pocket.

"Thanks for the recommendations for this book and future books, Pastor. I appreciate your guidance and thoughts."

Pastor Swan gave Jerry a smile and a thumbs up.

They finished the gazebo, left the Family Life Center, and met their wives at the church office.

Driving home from the church, Jerry turned to Madeline, "Babe, do we have any plans for this Thursday after work?"

"Nope, what do you want to do?"

"I want to meet with Beverly to work on the novel for a couple of hours at Local Foods."

"That is great timing! Make changes when ideas are fresh! You better not have any red meat at dinner on Thursday!"

"I will call her later tonight to see if she can meet."

THURSDAY AT LOCAL FOODS ON DUNSTAN, 5:15 P.M.

After ordering, Eva said, "Jennifer, it's nice weather so let's sit outside." They walked to the front of the restaurant to sit at the booths facing the Dunstan side at Local Foods.

Twirling order number 21 on their table, Eva asked Jennifer what Jimmie wanted for his meal.

"Girl, he wants a crunchy chicken sandwich with fries. What about Thomas?"

"Thomas wants the steak special. He needs just a plain salad, Jennifer. But since I am not cooking tonight. so be it!" Eva added with a smile.

THURSDAY, 5:30 P.M.

Eva turned and glanced toward the parking lot. Noticing a black Jeep and white Escalade arriving at the same time and parking next to each other, Eva locked her eyes on the vehicles.

"Eva, what are you staring at?"

"Wait for it . . . I am about to find out if this is who I think it is. Look at the GTJBC bumper stickers on both the Jeep and Escalade."

Jerry jumped out of the Escalade while he smiled and waved at the Jeep, where Beverly appeared smiling.

Jerry's cell phone rang with Facetime. "Hello, Babe, we got here at the same time!"

"Hi, Ole Handsome One! Please turn the phone around so I can see Beverly also."

Beverly, waving and smiling, replied, "Hello, Madeline. We got to get together for lunch next Saturday."

"Beverly, that is a date. Look, girl, please do not let that husband of mine work you to death this evening. The real reason I called is for you to make sure he does not get that steak special!"

Beverly blew her a kiss and winked, "I promise to be the food police!"

While still holding the phone and showing both of their faces for Madeline to see, Jerry grabbed Beverly's hands. He kissed them and held them up to show Madeline: "Wife, I am going to work these fingers to the bone." He kissed Beverly on both cheeks and added, "I am going to drain that brain. I want a *New York Times* Best Seller!"

Beverly squealed with laughter.

Madeline giggled, "Boy, you are so silly! And Beverly, you better find out where those lips have been before letting them touch you again. Your fingers and face might fall off!"

"Both of you are too much, Madeline. I promise to watch over the meal and the work time. They close at 9 anyway." Beverly, still laughing, blew a kiss and waved bye to Madeline.

"Bye y'all." Madeline hung up.

"Jennifer, you said it!" Eva rolled her eyes. "He is fooling around with a church member. And that's Beverly, the choir director's wife!"

Jennifer sneered, "Yep, that's the choir director's wife. What's his name?" Jennifer asked, patting her forehead with her palm. "What is his name? Uh, uh! I got it: Pastor Charles Smith, that's him. Look at them taking a selfie. Can you believe those adulterers are waving, smiling, and blowing kisses in their selfie?"

Slapping Jennifer's arm, Eva commented, "Girl, did you see him kissing her hands and lips in the selfie! Are they crazy? She is just laughing while committing adultery with somebody else's husband. That's a real sinner!!"

"Since he plans to divorce Madeline, neither one of them gives a fat rat. You know, she has a baby that's about a year old." Jennifer tapped the table. "I wonder if that's his baby and not Pastor Smith's?"

"Shut the front door!" Eva clapped her hands. "Do you think it's been going on that long between them?'

"Eva, you know I work in the nursery this Sunday. When she brings that baby into the nursery, I am going to take a good look to see who that baby really resembles!"

Eva got up, sat next to Jennifer facing the Local Foods Market, and said, "Let me sit next to you. That way my back is to them when they walk past us. They won't be able to see us. You know something, Jennifer: I am going to make sure I'm at church the Sunday Pastor Swan puts them under church discipline. He is going to get them good!! I feel so sorry for Madeline and Pastor Smith."

Out in the parking lot, Jerry opened the back of Beverly's Jeep and retrieved her laptop. "Whose choir robe are you hauling around?"

"Yours!" Beverly nodded her head at him.

"Mine?"

"Correct! The Right Reverend Dr. Charles Smith, your first cousin, told me to give you that robe and to tell you he 'knows you and your two cronies have missed two choir rehearsals and you three amigos are facing choir church discipline'! He also said next Sunday it's your turn to cook BBQ for the Sunday night Dallas Cowboys game, and he wants baby backs."

"Beverly, first, there are 'a thousand people' in our choir. How can he know the three of us have missed two rehearsals?"

"Jerry, have you forgotten he started us signing in at every rehearsal? The choir secretary gives him a report."

"Beverly, tell my cousin he gets hot dogs and as for choir rehearsal . . ."

Holding up her hands to interrupt and smiling, Beverly sang, "Um, tell him yourself!"

Jerry looked up at the sky before he opened the door. "Lord, why did you give us choir police who snitch?"

Beverly hit Jerry on the shoulder. "Boy, God's gonna get you. Let's eat and make these editing changes happen!"

Beverly and Jerry walked to the Market side of Local Foods to sit down.

"Eva, did you hear her say God's gonna get him? What did he say first? I couldn't hear him," Jennifer whispered.

"I didn't hear that part either. I wonder what makes her think God is not going to get her foolin' around tail!" Eva quipped.

Before placing their order, Jerry began updating Beverly about the book changes. "Pastor suggests that the couple does not divorce but goes into biblical counseling to work through their issues."

"Jerry, that can happen. I have completed Dr. Nicolas Ellen's biblical counseling training and supervision. I am a Certified Biblical Counselor. We can make the biblical counseling part in the book exactly right."

"Sister, that is awesome!" Jerry exclaimed.

While Beverly unpacked the laptop, Jerry went to order their meal.

SUNDAY MORNING

Sister Yvonne T, the women's Sunday school teacher for this Sunday at GTJBC, walked up to the mic. "Ladies, before we begin our lesson, please get in a group of three to pray, share prayer requests, and give praise reports."

Eva grabbed Jennifer's hand. "Come on!" They raced to include Madeline as their third person.

"Hi, ladies! How are you both?" Madeline greeted them cheerfully with a huge smile.

Eva gazed intently at Madeline. "We are fine . . . but how are you doing?"

"I am just fine!" Madeline still smiled brightly.

"Are you sure?" Eva questioned.

Looking puzzled, Madeline gazed at Eva. "Why would I not know how I am doing?"

"We do not want to be messy, so please come with us into the next room where it's quiet. The word is out: your husband is going to divorce you. We want to pray for you and your husband."

"Divorce! That's news to me," Madeline replied calmly.

Eva grabbed Madeline's hand, "Let's step outside."

They walked by several praying groups and entered the vacant room next door. Eva pushed a chair up to Madeline. "Please sit down."

Madeline smoothed the back of her green dress and sat.

"I hate to be the bearer of bad news, but I heard Jerry talking to Pastor Swan about divorcing you in eight months," Eva revealed.

"Also, Madeline, we saw your husband rendezvousing with Beverly Smith, the choir director's wife, this past Thursday at Local Foods on Dunstan. We saw him kiss Beverly on the lips twice and kiss her hands once in the parking lot while they were laughing and taking a selfie!" Jennifer added.

Madeline stood up. "Ladies, let me make sure I am getting this straight. Your names are . . . ?"

"I am Eva!"

"And I am Jennifer!"

"Eva and Jennifer," Madeline repeated.

They nodded solemnly.

"Ladies, thank you. I would like to pray. Please let's hold hands."
Madeline bowed her head, closed her eyes, and began praying:

"Father God, thank You for this day. Thank You, Father, so much
for giving us Your ways to manage and to solve messy life dramas,
messy life problems, messy life situations, and messy people.

"Father, thank You for this prayer time for the three of us. I ask
You to provide the three of us with Your wisdom to straighten out
and to stop in our church those who are Mess Creators, Mess
Containers, and Mess Carriers.

"Father, we want to prevent Future Messy Gossip, Future
Messy Misinterpretation, and Future Messy Misunderstandings.

"Father, in the Name of Jesus, please give me Your wisdom to
speak to Sisters Eva and Jennifer in a mature, open, loving, and
God-honoring reproving way."

(Eva nudged Jennifer and opened her eyes slightly to peep at
Madeline, whose eyes remained closed.)

"Father, my Lord, these Sisters Eva and Jennifer need Your
guidance to understand Proverbs 6: verses 16 to 19."

(Eva elbowed Jennifer again and opened her eyes wider to look at
Madeline, whose eyes remained closed. Jennifer peeped at Eva and
Madeline.)

"Lord, my husband Jerry is authoring a book and has been talking
about the characters in the book with Pastor Swan. In his book,
Jerry wanted a couple to divorce in eight months. Pastor Swan
disagreed with that because it would be reinforcing readers to

glamorize secular mess to deal with a couple's life problems rather than biblical counseling.

"Father, last Thursday Jerry and Sister Beverly were Facetiming me while they were at Local Foods Restaurant to meet about his book.

"My Lord, I saw my husband Jerry kiss Sister Beverly *once* on her cheeks and hands while they were on Facetime with me. They were not taking a selfie!

"Father God, please make it clear to all that Jerry and Sister Beverly are not in an adulterous relationship but rather a working relationship. She is his book editor.

"My Lord and Father, in Proverbs 6, You tell us how a lying person, devising wicked plans, running rapidly to evil and bearing false witness, is an abomination to you. Father, please place this in the hearts of Sisters Eva and Jennifer.

"Lord, please forgive my sisters who thought they were helping but have begun to create a messy situation and a messy misunderstanding based upon a messy interpretation.

"Father God, I forgive my sisters Eva and Jennifer."

(Madeline squeezed both their hands.)

"Father God, in the Name of Jesus, please give Sisters Eva and Jennifer Your wisdom so that when they are around to share any information, we will not have a reason to go at once to meditate on Ephesians 6 for your Word of protection.

"Father God, we love and praise You, thank You, and have faith in You and Your ways of dealing with all life issues to keep us from the world's messy ways. Thank You, Lord, in the Name of Jesus. Amen!"

Madeline opened her eyes, then hugged Eva and Jennifer. She smiled and, as she walked out the door, said, "Ladies, y'all please have a super blessed day! Now let's get back to Sunday school so we can all learn more about following our Lord from Dr. Ellen's book *Coming to Know and Walk with God,* rather than walking with mess and gossip."

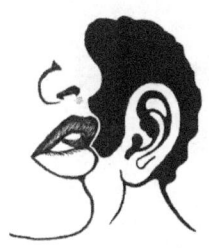

There's Always One!

Waving her left hand with note cards while holding the mic in her right, Sister Yvonne T began speaking. "Ladies, may I have your attention! Let's begin Sunday school. Please take a seat, and each of you take an index card and a pen from the box I will pass around. We have been studying Proverbs to get God-given wisdom. Today we are going to discuss and have fun with 'proverbs from our family that have stayed with us.'"

The forty ladies in the classroom began laughing. Sister Velma raised her hand to speak.

Yvonne T pointed at her. "Yes, Sister Velma."

Smiling and shrugging sheepishly, Velma asked, "What if some of the 'sayings or family proverbs,' as you put them, include salty language? How do you want that written and spoken? We are in the Lord's House!"

"Sister Velma, even if we were not in the Lord's House, we should make sure to 'not let any profane language come from our mouth.' But to answer your question, rather than use the profane words, insert the word *Bleep!* We will get the gist of the meaning." Sister Yvonne T nodded and continued, "Will that work for everybody?"

"Works for me!" Sister Velma gave a thumbs-up sign.

"Thank you, Sister Velma, for bringing that to our attention," Sister Yvonne T replied with a smile and a thumbs up in return.

"All right, ladies, please write two family proverbs that have been guidelines and guardrails for your life. We will share your family proverbs and then we will see how they align with God's Proverbs. We will allow about fifteen minutes to complete your writing tasks."

In the Sunday school room, the family proverbs assignment triggered laughter and comments like "You were told that too?" "Girl, I tell that to my children today!" "Can you believe that still holds true?" "I'll try to watch my mouth today after hearing that one!"

"Okay ladies, let's share!" Sister Yvonne T had to raise her voice to be heard. "Who wants to start?"

Sister Velma stood up, "I will. I had a mentor named Dr. P who said, 'Always remember where three or more and sometimes even two are assembled, there is likely to be one *Bleep* fool. Make sure that is not you!'" Velma repeated the sentence for emphasis, holding up three fingers.

Mary yelled from the side of the room, "Watch out y'all! There are about forty of us in this room! So, who's the *Bleep* 'fool' in this room today?"

Everybody in the room pointed to Mary and began giggling.

Pointing her index finger to sweep from one side of the room to the other, Mary dissolved into laughter while trying to say, "So my sisters in Christ got judgmental, accusatory jokes! I am going to check with Pastor Swan to see if this is probable cause for church discipline."

Sister Velma looked at Mary and said, "You asked who the *Bleep* fool is and we answered you!"

Wiping tears from her eyes, Sister Yvonne T pounded the small podium at her side. When that didn't quiet the shouts of laughter and exclamations, she began speaking into the mic while waving her hands in the air. "Ladies, please let us return to order!"

Then, struggling to get control of her own giggles, Sister Yvonne T asked, "Who's going next?"

Pops in the Hospital

Rita and Robert, both in their sixties, grew up in a close-knit family. As sister and brother they were best friends since childhood.

Rita's husband Larry and Robert's wife Faye often discussed and laughed at the stories they heard about their spouses from Rosalyn (Moms) and Roger (Pops)—Rita's and Robert's parents.

Rita's and Robert's mother Rosalyn (Moms) transitioned at the age of ninety, two years ago.

Their father Roger (Pops) lost his vision a decade ago. At the age of ninety-five, he had lived with Rita and her husband Larry since his wife's death.

Pops, known as an easygoing man who loved his family, retained the same easygoing attitude after becoming blind.

Larry described his father-in-law as a "fun and entertaining man to live with."

Robert and his wife Faye are very attentive to Pops. They help his sister Rita and Larry in the care of Pops. Robert spends time at Rita and Larry's house with Pops. Robert also brings Pops to his and Faye's home for weekly visits to give Rita and Larry a break.

One cloudy Friday afternoon, Robert received a phone call, and seeing the caller ID, Robert knew it was Rita. "Yes, my dear sister, how may I serve you?"

"Robert, Pops keeps complaining about stomach pains! We are taking him to Methodist Emergency Center on Kirby."

"Faye and I will meet you guys over there. Is he able to walk on his own?"

"Yeah, Larry is walking him out to the car."

"Okay, we will see you and Pops soon."

METHODIST EC WAITING ROOM
FRIDAY AFTERNOON

Entering the waiting room, Robert and Faye saw Larry motioning them to join him.

"Rita is back there with Pops. She just sent this text: 'The doctor has ordered x-rays of his stomach and abdomen.'"

Robert texted Rita: "We are here. What is the initial impression?"

Rita immediately replied: "The doc is waiting to get blood work results and to see the x-rays. I will come out in a minute to let you be in here to see him. He is talking and asking questions about what is happening."

Rita walked into the waiting room and hugged Robert. "The Tech is doing the x-ray, so I had to step out of the room. Give them a couple of minutes before you go back, bro."

Faye stepped toward them with a look of concern and compassion. "Rita, how is he doing?"

"He is in pain, but you know he tries not (using air quotes) 'to cause unnecessary drama.'"

Faye, smiling through misty eyes and hugging Rita, replied, "That's our Pops."

After another minute, Robert left the waiting room to see Pops.

"Hi Pops, how are you feeling?"

"Hi son. I have a little pain that won't go away here on my right side."

The doctor walked into the room. "Hi, I was talking to Mr. Harper's daughter earlier. You are . . . ?"

Looking at her ID badge, Robert replied, "Dr. Wright, I am Robert, Mr. Harper's son. My sister and I take care of Pops. What is going on with him?"

Pops waved his hand to get their attention. "Excuse me! I am over here and need to know what's happening."

"Sorry, Mr. Harper, after looking at your . . ."

Robert held up his hand to stop the doctor. "I hate to interrupt you, but may I get my sister on the phone to hear?"

"Ask your sister to come back. I will allow both of you here to listen to what I tell your father."

After receiving Robert's text, Rita arrived and went to hold Pop's right hand.

"Mr. Harper, your appendix is creating your pain. We will transfer you by ambulance to the hospital, where you will have an appendectomy," Dr. Wright stated.

"A what?" Pops' voice trembled slightly.

"Sorry, Mr. Harper. The surgeon at the hospital will take out your appendix today," the doctor explained.

"Today?!" Pops raised his head quickly.

"Yes, sir. When an appendix is acting up like yours, it must come out quickly."

"I see," Pops replied more calmly.

"Pops, I will ride in the ambulance with you, okay?" Robert asked while patting his father on his legs.

"That's good, son. Where's Rita?"

"I'm here, Pops. I just stepped away to let Dr. Wright get closer to you."

METHODIST HOSPITAL SURGERY FLOOR
FRIDAY EVENING

Dr. Mathis, the surgeon, spoke to Robert, Rita, Faye, and Larry. "This surgery will take about one hour."

Dr. Walker, the anesthesiologist, added, "Your dad will have general anesthesia. At his age, side effects might be some temporary confusion and memory loss, dizziness, and difficulty urinating."

"You did say *temporary*, right?" Robert responded.

"If he has any of these side effects, they will more than likely be very temporary because, thank goodness, your father is in good health for his age. We are taking him away right now."

Robert said, "Wait—we need to pray before you go, Pops."

"Thanks, son. You know I must be in His hands and care first."

"Our Father, we thank you for being our ever-present Help and Protector. Please bless my father as he undergoes surgery. You said You would not leave or forsake us and that You are always with us. Please let my father feel and know Your Presence during his surgery. And please provide protection, guidance, wisdom, and peace to all the medical staff taking care of Pops. In the Name of Jesus, we pray, Amen."

Squeezing Robert's hand and getting drowsy from the medication, Pops mumbled, "Amen! Thanks, son."

"Pops, we will be here when you get back!" Robert and Rita gave him a kiss on his forehead.

Beginning to fall asleep, Pops gave a thumbs-up sign.

Robert said, "Sis, I will spend tonight and the other nights with him if you want to take the daytimes. If all goes well, the docs believe he will be going home in about three to four days."

"That will work. Thank you, Baby Bro."

METHODIST HOSPITAL
SATURDAY MORNING

Rita arrived and entered Pops' room. "Good morning, Harper men. How are the sick and the shut in?"

Robert was helping Pops to sip water.

"Hi Sis. He is doing well. He's just a little groggy and weak."

Pops waved and closed his eyes.

Rita whispered, "I will take it from here. See you later, bro. Go eat and get some sleep."

"See you tonight around 9. Let me know what the docs say."

METHODIST HOSPITAL
SATURDAY NIGHT

As Robert returned, Rita reported, "Pops is more alert and did good sipping on the broth. He just dozed off to sleep. I texted you that the doc said he is doing well and recovering at the expected pace."

Smiling at the encouragement, Robert responded, "I saw that. Let me walk you to your car."

She replied, "No need; I didn't drive. Larry is coming to pick me up. I called him when you texted you were here."

Robert eventually fell asleep in the room's recliner. Suddenly he heard Pops yelling, "Robert, look at that man on the crane holding a gun!"

"What? A man with a gun?" Robert jumped up and ran to the window. "Pops, I don't see a crane or man!"

"Keeping looking, Robert—I know what I saw!" Pops shouted.

Robert started shaking his head, grinning, and muttering to himself. "What in the world am I doing? Why am I looking for a man with a gun outside this window? Pops is blind and cannot see his hands in front of his face. How can he see a man outside this window?!"

Chuckling and bending down to his father's bedside, Robert patted his shoulder. "Pops, yes sir, you saw a man, but you were dreaming!"

Glasses and Sneezes

L et me use your reading glasses," Sandra requested and held out her hands to Becky.

"Where are your glasses? Don't answer. That's about the fiftieth pair you have lost this month!" Becky replied, while removing her own glasses and handing them to Sandra.

"Girl, I know. I am glad I go to the dollar stores to get the reading specs. It does not matter then if I lose them."

"Sandra, you have spent a small fortune on reading glasses from the dollar store. I bet you would keep up with a pair of readers if you spent some real money on them." Becky giggled while making a dollar sign.

"For your information, I have an eye appointment next Tuesday at the Alkek Eye Center. I think I will get me a good pair of readers. I will just die if I lose a pair of $100 glasses!"

TUESDAY

Becky looked at her Apple Watch and hit the answer icon. "Hello, Sister Sandra. How did the eye appointment go?"

"I will be the owner of a $250 pair of readers within a week. To be honest, I almost died when I got that price. That tech was trying to talk me into a $300 pair. I drew the line at that!"

"Sister, over the years you've spent that much on buying all the lost glasses that just cost $1. Anyway, I bet your 'happy behind' will keep up with those $100 glasses."

Laughing, Sandra exclaimed, "Excuse me, Miss Becky: the cost is $250!"

ALKEK EYE CENTER

The technician straightened the yellow reading glasses on Sandra's nose and gave her a card to read. "Please read the last line on this card for me."

"The big brown dog is wagging his tail from left to right."

"Great! Do you like the way your glasses feel and look, Ms. Smith?"

"I do. I love this yellow and like the way they fit down on my nose. The small size of the lens is exactly right. I can easily see over these lenses when I'm not reading, while these glasses rest on my nose." Sandra turned her head side to side while admiring her new look in the mirror.

"Okay, I am glad you like them and can read well with them!" The technician reached out to remove the readers from Sandra's face.

Sandra drew back and put her hand up to block the technician. "I am going to keep them on my nose to get used to them, and this yellow is a cute match with my dress."

"That's fine. Here is the readers' storage pouch."

Sandra took the black pouch and smiled. "Thank you, Mr. Sam. You have given me excellent service."

"You are welcome, Ms. Smith. If you have any problems, please come back. And make sure you keep your annual eye exam."

"I will." Sandra got up from the table and gave a final glance in the mirror.

Then she walked out the door and down the steps, stopping to Facetime Becky.

"Hey, girl! Are those the new ones?" Becky asked.

"Yes, indeedy! Don't I look cute?!" Sandra began walking and turned to enter the parking lot.

"I must admit they look chic." Becky gave a thumbs up.

While waiting on the curb for a car to pass, Sandra touched the left earpiece of her readers and smiled into her phone screen. "Yep, they look great!"

Sandra then began sneezing. Her glasses fell off her nose and slid into the large storm drain below the curb.

Stunned and in disbelief over the disappearance of her $250 glasses, Sandra stared intently at the gutter.

Becky noticed Sandra's glasses were missing and yelled, "What just happened?"

Sandra grabbed a yard-long stick lying in the gutter and began poking it into the drain.

Noticing her unusual "fishing" efforts, the parking-lot attendant walked up. "Ma'am, may I help you with something?"

"I wish you could help get my $250 glasses back," Sandra replied sadly.

"Ma'am, what happened and where are they?"

Pointing with the stick toward the drain, Sandra answered, "Down there."

"How did that happen?"

Regretfully giving up her retrieval attempt, she tossed the stick back into the gutter. "I just got my glasses, walked out with them on my nose, sneezed, and they fell down that black hole!"

"Ma'am, are you kidding me?" He tried to hold back a smile.

"Sandra, no way! Please tell me you are joking!" Becky yelled.

Looking at her phone and at the attendant, Sandra sighed. "Nope, I wish this was only a joke!"

The attendant covered his mouth and choked out the muffled words, "Ma'am, I am sorry for your loss." He then walked quickly away, his shoulders shaking from laughter.

"Becky, I'll call you back later. I got to go back to the dollar store to buy reading glasses!" Sandra grimly disconnected the call.

It's Always about Hair

Volunteers from Going To Jesus Bible Church daily clean the church building, Family Life Center/School, and the church offices.

Kathy and Ellen are friends who have the sanctuary cleanup assignment every other Saturday.

Kathy turned off the vacuum cleaner and yelled to her friend. "Hey Ellen! Let us go to Local Foods when we finish. I've invited my coworker Ashley to join us. She started working at my office about six months ago."

"Great! I am craving the vegan taco salad," Ellen answered.

As they entered the Local Foods door, Kathy saw Ashley sitting at the table in front. Ashley got up and gave Kathy a hug. "Hi Kathy. How was the cleanup morning?"

"It went fast. This is my friend Ellen."

"It's nice to meet you. At work, Kathy talks about y'all's shopping mishaps and political concerns all the time," Ashley said, smiling in greeting.

"Oh My Goodness! I hope my blabbermouth friend does not tell all about our shopping behavior!" Ellen said, while laughing and moving her hair twists to the back of her head.

"Let's go order!" Kathy began walking to open the door. "Yep, I have told all you have done to make salespeople nuts!"

"Me! Well, my friend. I pray the Holy Spirit pricks your heart!" Ellen retorted, walking past Kathy.

While they ate and chatted, Ellen noticed that Ashley kept glancing at her hair. Ellen had to make a conscious effort to ignore Ashley's obvious interest in her hair.

Kathy stood up. "Ladies, I'm going to get more tea. Do either of you want anything to drink?"

"I'm good," Ellen replied.

"No, but thank you," Ashley shook her head.

"I will be back in one minute." Kathy picked up her plastic glass and walked toward the drink bar.

"Ellen, how long have you had your hair like that?" Ashley asked.

"For several years. Why are you asking about my hair?" Ellen narrowed her eyes in puzzlement.

Kathy had returned and sat down next to Ellen.

"Ellen, is all that your real hair, or do you have store-bought hair mixed in?" Ashley asked in a subtly insulting tone.

With disgust and irritation, Kathy held her palm up to stop Ellen's reply. Kathy then got up and pulled off her own shoulder-length blonde wig, exposing her bald head, the result of cancer treatment.

Ashley jumped and looked startled.

Kathy glared at Ashley and demanded, "Why are you asking Ellen about her hair, and you have never questioned me about whether this is all my hair?" Kathy held the blonde wig a few inches from Ashley's face.

"I am sorry. I did not mean anything by asking." Ashley stared and bobbed her head between Kathy's bald head and the blonde wig Kathy kept waving in her face.

"Microaggression at its best, Ashley! I will certainly share this with my students when I teach my Community Health Worker class in a few weeks. Dog! I hate I did not have my phone video to record your microaggression in real time," Kathy spoke firmly.

Ellen smiled, stood up, and said, "Kathy, as usual you are a hoot. I will see you in the car, my friend."

Ellen walked toward the door and stopped. She returned to the table, gently held Ashley's right hand like a mother holds a child's hand, and looked into Ashley's blue eyes.

Ashley jumped when Ellen took her hand.

"Do not be scared, Miss Ashley. I am not going to hurt you. You are blessed that the Holy Spirit spoke to me. Sugar, you and 'your kind' need to examine the reasons you are constantly obsessing over and concerned about African Americans', Black folks', hair. 'Your kind' have a need to touch Black babies' hair. Your kind aggressively target Black children in schools and adults in the workplace with demands to stop wearing or to cut off braids, dreads, and big afros."

Patting Ashley's hand, Ellen continued. "Baby, your kind's obsession and focus on Black folks' hair is troubling because that's very unnatural behavior. Please seek professional help, and encourage others like you to do likewise." Ellen gently placed Ashley's hand back on the table.

Ellen looked at Kathy and began laughing. "Kathy, please put your hair back on your head. Let's head to the car, Sistah." Ellen gave Kathy a hug.

Ellen then yelled, "Hey Miss Ashley!"

Ashley jerked her head up to look at Ellen.

Ellen signed while saying "love, peace, and soul to you" and walked out the door.

The Wrong Man Today!

Men from Going To Jesus Bible Church were in ten groups of ten, hanging up health-fair signs and completing other chores around the church grounds. Pastor Swan and the men used times like this to fellowship and "cut up" with each other.

Elder Smith called to Pastor Swan, "Doc, we are out of zip ties. You and Brother Williams are signed up as the gofers for our group."

Pastor Swan swatted Brother Williams on the shoulder and smiled. "Let's go, Brother Williams. We'll take the scenic route to Walmart!"

"Doc, we need you both back in about thirty-five minutes, please sir!" Elder Smith retorted.

Pastor Swan and Brother Williams dropped the signs they were carrying and started walking toward the church parking lot.

Elder Smith yelled, "Hey gentlemen!"

Both men turned around.

Elder Smith exhorted, "No stopping by Specs!"

"Now you got jokes!" Brother Williams commented, grinning.

Pastor Swan laughed and gave Elder Smith a Cross sign, yelling, "Get behind us righteous men, satan!"

While at Walmart, Pastor Swan turned to Brother Williams and said, "Will you go get the zip ties while I pick up a few snacks for all the men to munch on before we head to the big group meal later this afternoon. Meet me at the self-checkout registers. That reminds me: I need to buy biscuits to take home. I'll see you in a few minutes."

Brother Williams replied, "Got it!"

After shopping successfully, they met at the self-checkout. Pastor Swan scanned, bagged, and paid for the items. They each carried a bag outside.

As they walked toward Pastor Swan's black Silverado truck, a man in a blue hoodie approached the pastor, pulled a 9mm gun, and pointed it at Pastor Swan's head. "Give me your wallet now, preacher man!"

"Snap! You noticed my collar!" the pastor replied as he searched the hooded man's eyes.

"Shut your preacher man's mouth and give me your wallet before I blow off your preacher collar and your brains out in front of your boy here," yelled the hooded man.

Pastor Swan said okay and dropped the bag of groceries in front of the gunman.

When the bag hit the ground, two loud popping sounds startled the gunman, who glanced down at the bag. Two cans of biscuits had exploded.

Taking advantage of the distraction, Pastor Swan stepped back and knocked the gunman to the ground with three rapid side-kicks.

Walmart security arrived and started trying to push through the small crowd that had gathered.

Pastor Swan in seconds pulled the gunman's hands up, held them while he quickly flipped the gunman onto his stomach, and said, "Williams, give me a large zip tie. And cover that gun with your foot so no one else gets hurt!"

Brother Williams, initially standing with open mouth in shock from the pastor's martial arts skills, located the gun and stepped on it. Then he tore into the zip-tie bag and gave one to Pastor Swan.

The gunman began bucking and trying to get away from the pastor, who then put the gunman in a scissor hold, zip-tied his hands behind him, and stepped hard on the gunman's right leg.

The gunman screamed in pain. Pastor Swan said sternly, "Keep yelling and I will pin your other leg too!"

The surrounding crowd began cheering and clapping. A security guard finally shoved through the crowd and pulled a gun on Pastor Swan. "Get up and put your hands up!"

The pastor followed his commands. Brother Williams handed the guard the 9mm.

The security guard looked at Pastor Swan and demanded, "Do you have another gun on you?"

Brother Williams replied, "Man, you got your gun on the wrong person. That guy on the ground just got his behind kicked after he put that gun I gave you in my pastor's face. That gun belongs to the crying, wannabe tough man on the ground. He's tied up because he tried to rob the wrong man!"

The crowd began yelling comments: "Get your gun off him. Arrest that criminal there on the ground! Man, you got your gun on the victim! Stop being stupid!!"

Two Stafford police arrived and pushed through the crowd. Officer Jones yelled, "Excuse us, please step back."

The officer, startled when he saw Pastor Swan with his hands up in the air, said, "Hey, Pastor Swan, what is going on?"

Officer Jones then turned to the security guard and ordered, "Man, take that gun off Pastor Swan! Pastor, please put your hands down!"

The security guard opened his mouth to speak, but Officer Jones held up both hands to quiet him.

Then Officer Jones recognized Brother Williams. "Williams, how are you? What's happening?"

"I'm good." Brother Williams pointed to the hooded man on the ground. "But this ignorant clown came up, put that 9mm gun in Pastor's face, and demanded his wallet. Pastor Swan took this punk out! Man, you should have seen Pastor's moves!"

The hooded man began yelling louder, "I need help! He broke my leg!"

"Shut up! We just might stand back and let the pastor really break your leg for trying to rob him! He just pinned you down by stepping on that boney leg! Stand up, your leg is not broke!" Officer Jones shouted back.

The officer took the 9mm gun from the security guard and peered at the hooded man: "Is this your gun?"

Silence.

"Your fingerprints are on the gun, dummy. You don't have to answer. We'll match you to this weapon!" Officer Jones snarled.

Then he looked at his partner Officer Rice and said, "Book him, Rice-O!"

"I need to get to the hospital, not jail! I'm hurt!" whined the hooded man.

"Shut up, dummy; we will get your leg looked at!" Officer Jones yelled and then started laughing. "You picked the wrong man to try to rob today!"

"Pastor, you and Williams go on. We will be in touch when it's court time for Mr. Dummy!"

"The show is over! Please move on!" Officer Rice yelled to the small crowd.

Brother Williams looked at his buzzing phone. "Pastor, this is Elder Smith."

"Tell him we were held up with a situation and will be back shortly," Pastor Swan replied calmly.

After Brother Williams hung up from the call, he looked at Pastor Swan. "Man, where did you learn martial arts skills like that?"

Pastor Swan smiled. "If I tell you, I'll have to kill you!"

"Man, you are tough!" Brother Williams nodded seriously at the pastor.

"Navy Seals. Now let's see what we need to go back into Walmart to rebuy," Pastor Swan commented.

The Handicap Tag

Merial and Rose have been best friends since childhood. After graduating high school, Merial went to undergraduate school in Nashville. Rose stayed at home in Rome, Georgia, to attend college.

One day they met for lunch at Krystal on Turner McCall, their favorite meeting and eating place.

Merial shook her head. "Nope, I am done with college. You help yourself to graduate school!"

"Okay, I'm heading to Knoxville for two years!" Rose hit Merial's arm.

"Go right ahead. I will be here or near ATL when you get back from getting more educated!" Merial picked up her Krystal hamburger and took a bite.

ON THE PHONE THIRTY YEARS LATER

"Merial, my best friend, it's Rose. I'm calling you from Mom's house. I am going back to Austin tomorrow afternoon, since Mom is better.

I need to get back to work. What time are you coming to Rome to drop me at the airport?"

"I will be there around ten in the morning. My friend Agnes is coming with me. We'll take you to lunch before dropping you at the airport. Tell Mom PG hello for me!"

Rose looked at her mom, known as PG. "Your Number Two Daughter says hello."

"Hello, My Baby Girl!" Rose's mom yelled toward the cell phone.

"Are we going to Krystal before I leave?" Rose asked Merial.

"No ma'am! We have another place to eat in mind. It's new in College Park," Merial replied.

"Great—see you in the morning."

TRIP TO THE AIRPORT

Merial, Agnes, and Rose headed toward Rockmart to go to College Park on Highway 278.

Agnes said, "Rose, Merial told me you both have been friends since childhood."

"Yep, we have. Some days in elementary school, we would meet to walk to the store to buy a Coke, and other days, we'd get a Double Cola and sip on the drink together while walking home. We did this until integration separated us in the school system. But we stayed connected, as you can see."

Agnes pulled the visor down, began primping her hair, and said, "Now this is a real friendship. We will be at the restaurant in a few minutes, Rose."

Merial giggled, "Who are you are trying to fix up to see at this place?"

Agnes quickly pointed to the handicap tag hanging on Merial's rear-view mirror. "Girl, please! I couldn't get a man to look at me if I wanted to, no matter how I try to fix up while riding in this car! You always keep this handicap thing visible. This hang-tag is telling any eligible man that something is very wrong with one if not all of us in this car!"

Agnes laughed and turned to look at Rose, who had joined in the laughter. "I tell Merial to remove this hang-tag when we are out, but no, no, no! She keeps this thing visible, so it can send this message, 'Women with issues! Beware!!'"

Merial chuckled and swatted Agnes's left arm. "I'm leaving you at this restaurant today! Many of us, my dear friend, need this handicap tag and are not ashamed of our limitations or to show we have them. Be thankful to God that you can get around and park wherever you want, without needing a handicap tag—and that I'm determined to stay your friend in spite of your attitude!"

Rose hit Merial on her shoulder, clapped, and said "Amen!"

Communion Supplies for the Cowboys' Playoff

Roger, a senior student at the University of Houston, enjoyed attending Going To Jesus Bible Church and spending time being mentored by the Elders at the church.

Roger had a close bond with Elder Michael, and as they talked together, he learned about serving in the Armed Services. Elder Michael had spent more than twenty years in the Air Force before retiring. Roger was planning to join the Air Force after graduation.

Also, Roger and his wife Michelle enjoyed going to Elder Michael's home to watch their favorite football team, the Dallas Cowboys. Because this week's game was on Monday, they decided to remain home and phone Elder Michael, whom they called "Uncle Mike."

Preparing for the Monday night wild-card playoff game, Elder Michael just completed setting his food tray in front of the TV and was walking to the kitchen when the phone rang, announcing "Call from Michelle."

"Hello Uncle Mike. This Michelle."

"Hey, I know who this is. My phone announced you," Elder Michael replied. "Have you and Roger turned on the game?"

"Yes sir! We are ready. Do you have your prayers ready to pray the Cowboys to a win?" Michelle asked, snickering.

"Michelle, I have more than prayers tonight. I also have my Communion supplies together!"

Michelle let out a loud squeal after his comment.

Roger ran into their den, looking worried after hearing the squeal, and was relieved when he saw Michelle laughing. "Who is that and what is going on?"

Michelle then handed the phone to Roger.

"Hello and who is this?" Roger demanded.

"Hey man, this is Elder Michael. What happened to Michelle?"

"She has lost it laughing. What did you say to her?"

"Nothing—except in preparation for the game tonight, I felt a need to include Communion supplies along with the much-needed prayers for a win," he repeated.

Roger chuckled. "Uncle Mike, you are too much!"

"Man, look at your phone and you will see the Communion supplies!"

"Michelle, you have got to come see Uncle Mike's pic of his Communion supplies for tonight's game!" Roger guffawed, hard enough to draw tears from his eyes.

Michelle looked at the pic, and out came another loud squeal.

Elder Michael chuckled, "Y'all get off the phone; the game has started. Let's do a halftime check-in. Blessings, my children!" Elder Michael hung up.

Roger and Michelle continued their tearful laughter as they settled in front of the TV. They made sure to have Roger's phone nearby, so they could refer to the Communion supplies pic if the game started looking like the Cowboys needed extra Help.

My Aunties, the Funeral Ushers

THURSDAY

While adjusting the Facetime view on her iPhone, Ester began speaking with her usual bright smile. "Now I can see you better, my friend. Amy, are you and Reg coming to join us for dinner and a movie tomorrow?"

"Reg and I have plans to come, but who is *us*?" Amy questioned.

"The two loves of my life, my twin Aunties Mar and Joy, the funeral crashers-ushers!"

Amy grinned. "Why do you call them that anyway? I don't believe I've ever heard you explain that."

Chuckling, Ester replied, "Girl, when you and Reg come, I will introduce them to you guys and explain their titles. See y'all tomorrow night!"

"Wait, before you hang up, Ester! That music sounds super! Who is that playing the sax?"

"Grady Gaines Douglas is an excellent saxophonist. I will let you and Reg hear the entire album, *The Power of Agape Love,* or you can just download it. You will a*gape* love it!" Ester replied excitedly.

FRIDAY NIGHT DINNER AND A MOVIE

When the doorbell rang, Ester looked at her phone and saw Amy and Reg standing at the door. Speaking into her phone, "I have unlocked the door, come on in," Ester locked the door after hearing it close.

Walking into the kitchen, Amy went to Ester's right and Reg went to the left. Simultaneously they kissed Ester on both cheeks.

"Thanks, peeps! I'm almost done here with the salad mix that will complement my awesome spaghetti!"

"Where are the Aunties?" Reg asked.

Ester pointed to her phone. "Walking up to the door as you speak."

Before Amy could leave the kitchen to open the door, Auntie Mar began speaking into the camera, while pushing the Ring doorbell with her thumb. "Baby girl, open the door! We know you can hear and see us with this contraption."

Using her iPhone, Ester opened and then locked the door after her Aunties entered.

"Aunties, we are in the kitchen!"

Smiling, Ester's seventy-year-old identical twin Aunties Mar and Joy removed their scarves simultaneously from their braided grey hair, exposing their wrinkle-free, dark brown skin. Both Aunties held their arms open, reaching to hug Ester.

"Hi My Lovelies!" Ester hugged and kissed each aunt while pointing to Amy and Reg. "Here are Amy and Reg, Aunties. They will hang with us tonight."

"Hi," Auntie Mar and Joy said in unison, and each gave Amy and Reg a hug.

"I see what we are eating, but what is the movie?" Auntie Mar went to the sink to wash her hands, and Auntie Joy followed.

"We are watching *The Woman King*," Ester answered.

"Great! I heard some good stuff about that movie. Isn't it still at the movies? How are we going to see it? Girl, don't steal movies. I'm too old for jail!" Auntie Joy exclaimed.

Amy, Reg, and Ester began laughing. "Auntie Joy, I am paying to watch the movie here!" Amy replied.

"Oh my! This is a new movie-watching day!" Auntie Joy said, chuckling.

Waving his hand in the air to get their attention, Reg asked, "Please tell Amy and me why your niece calls you funeral crashers-ushers?"

"Oh, so that is our nickname behind our back!" Auntie Mar said, while giving Ester the side eye.

"Don't act like you two don't volunteer to usher at every funeral held at Going To Jesus Bible Church or to show up as usher backups, even when you are not needed!" Ester snickered.

Auntie Joy grinned. "Okay, you got us! We are serving as ushers and loving on people as ushers, like good Christians."

"Reg and Amy, the best drama shows are at funerals. It's like being at *Saturday Night Live* in real time! People fight, faint, drink, sleep, romance, lie, pretend, and connive, to name a few. There are some genuine carryings-on at many funerals." Auntie Mar cackled while putting spaghetti on her plate.

Then she gestured at Auntie Joy. "My Sister is not as amused as I am when the drama begins. She just watches with disbelief."

Joy looked pointedly at Mar. "As ushers when we are sent to remove flowers for the mortician, my sister here makes it a point to go and examine each body in the casket before getting the flowers. And later she critiques (mostly to me but often to the family) the casket and the way the deceased person looks. Last week at Elder Moore's funeral, Mar told his wife, 'Now y'all did right the way you put him away, and he looks like he has never been ill a day in his life. I am going to keep praying for the family.' I gently kicked her, pulled her away from the Elder's wife, and put a flower in her hand to take to the mortician staff."

Reg, Amy, Ester, and Auntie Mar's smiles gave way to loud laughter.

Ester held up her fork to get Reg and Amy's attention, while saying, "Wait, wait . . . let me tell you about these two 'borderline diabetics.' They told the head usher that, being diabetic, they need to occasionally nibble on snacks and sip on liquids. They made a plan with him so they could do so discreetly in the corner on the back pew while on funeral usher duties."

Auntie Mar started giggling and said, "Girl, stop running your mouth!"

Turning her back to Auntie Mar, Ester joined in the giggles. "The diabetic supplies? Their huge handbags conceal popcorn in containers and Cokes they carry to funerals, especially when they expect drama. When the fireworks begin, these two just snack away and sip on Coke while they watch funeral drama unfold in the church!"

Reg's head went down on the table and Amy's head fell backward as their loud laugher filled the room.

Snickering, Aunties Mar and Joy began shaking their index fingers at Ester. At the same time both warned, "Girl, we are going to beat your butt for running your mouth!"

"Why? You both know I am telling my best friends the truth!" Ester returned to eating while laughing.

Picking up his glass of red wine, Reg requested, "Aunties, please tell me what went on at the last funeral with drama where you two brought snacks to the church."

Joy snickered. "Go ahead, Mar; you tell it. You know you want to!"

"Last month Brother James died. Red must have been Brother James' favorite color. His casket was red, and he was dressed in a red suit. His family, wife Dorothy, and their two grown sons Adam and Rick, along with their wives, all wore red pantsuits. Before the mortician closed the casket, Dorothy got up and stood over his casket crying and screaming, 'Please come back! Please don't go!' While she was standing there screaming, Brother James' 'Chick on the Side' walked through the church doors and stood looking down the aisle at Dorothy. That 'Chick on the Side' was dressed to kill in a skintight red dress with two side splits up to her hips that showed her red lace panties!"

"You are joking, Auntie Mar!" Amy squealed.

"Nope, this the truth!" Auntie Joy interjected while shaking her head and tut tutting.

"Back to the funeral!" Auntie Mar demanded with a grin. "When the 'Chick on the Side' walked into the church, I whispered to Joy to move to the corner and get the snacks ready. Y'all, I knew a fight was about to happen. I kicked Elder Smith, who was sleeping on the back pew. I nodded toward that slinky red dress and then toward the wife who was still standing over the casket screaming.

"It did not take Elder Smith long to snap to the drama about to go down. He stood up and whispered in the ear of Usher Johnson, who looked up from his cell phone to see the 'Chick on the Side.' Usher Johnson dropped his phone and funeral programs on the floor. He quickly picked up his phone and began texting, leaving the programs scattered on the floor. Both men moved down the right aisle, slowly walking to the front of the church to get to Pastor Swan. Joy and I crossed our legs, leaned back in our corner on the last pew, and started discreetly eating our popcorn."

Laughing and taking a fortifying drink of his wine, Reg said, "Oh Aunties! Y'all are too much!"

"Back to the funeral again," Auntie Mar continued. "The 'Chick' began a slow, bouncy, hip-swiveling stroll toward Brother James' wife and the casket. Her long red wig made swinging sweeps on her back with every step.

"As the 'Chick on the Side' took her hip-swinging bounce down the church's center aisle, heads began turning to look at her. People started whispering and looking from Brother James' wife to Brother James' 'Chick' approaching. Dorothy had not noticed that slinky red dress swiveling nearer."

Amy looked at Auntie Joy, who sipped her wine between chuckles. "Auntie Joy, what were you saying and doing during this drama?"

"I was enjoying the popcorn with the sips of Coke and told Mar we needed more than Coke for this! And we did! We also needed some of this stuff!" Auntie Joy pointed to her wine glass.

Reg and Amy both choked on their spaghetti.

"Didn't I tell y'all these two are a mess!" Ester commented.

"Well y'all, before the 'Chick on the Side' reached Brother James' wife at the casket," Auntie Mar continued, "Dorothy's sister Tammy stood up and reached for the Chick's shoulder to stop her. Tammy's hands missed the shoulder and instead grabbed the red wig. Off came the wig to reveal a black-stocking-cap-covered head!"

Auntie Mar sipped her wine. "The 'Chick on the Side' covered her head with her hands and screamed. That scream got Dorothy's attention, so she turned and saw the Chick. Before anybody could stop Dorothy, she sprinted down the center aisle. She kicked down the Chick, grabbed her by the back of her dress, and began dragging her toward the door at the back of the church. The Chick was kicking and screaming, 'You better let me go, you ole heifer!' Y'all, before any of the men could get to Dorothy, she straddled the Chick, balled up her big fist, and knocked out the Chick! Dorothy looked down at the knocked-out woman and yelled, 'This ole heifer just let you go!'

"Pastor Swan ran to the pulpit to stop the funeral and asked everyone to remain seated. Elder Jones arranged for an ambulance to take the Chick to the hospital. Along with Pastor Swan and Dorothy's family members, Dorothy was escorted to the pastor's office."

Waving a piece of garlic bread in the air, Auntie Joy interjected,

"After about thirty minutes we ushers were summoned to the outside of the sanctuary into the vestibule and were told that Dorothy requested to continue the funeral. Mar and I were asked to hold open the sanctuary doors. Walking in front of Dorothy and family, Pastor Swan led the dressed-in-red family entourage back into the sanctuary. Dorothy and her family took their front-row seats. Pastor Swan walked to the pulpit and gave a five-minute eulogy."

"Yep, that was the first fast eulogy Pastor Swan has ever given and, we hope, the only live one-way Chick fight we ever see with snacks at Going To Jesus Bible Church!" Auntie Mar set her empty wine glass down on the table with a clink to mark the end of their story.

Cheering and laughing, Reg, Amy, and Ester stood and applauded the Aunties' recap of their funeral adventure.

www.ingramcontent.com/pod-product-compliance
Lightning Source LLC
Chambersburg PA
CBHW050412030726
47503CB00006B/2160